# The Ladoo Crew

# The Ladoo Crew

## Feminist Fables from The Chai House

### Priti Srivastava

This book is dedicated to those who have experienced a magical friendship with a member of the family Felidae.

# Contents

# Part One

# Chapter One

Anand crawled to one of his favorite spots. It was one of the closest ones, a location where he could still see the lean-to he had fashioned together as a place to stay dry and a little bit warmer. A spot where he could lay down and spread out, taking up as much space as he wanted on the forest floor, staring up at the clouds or when the clouds felt like parting, the starry skies. As he crawled towards the ferns, he couldn't stop thinking about their spiral, excited to take in their detail up close, to feel them on his fingertips. It felt like he had been watching them slowly unfurl for years. But it really must have only been days. He had only left three days ago, right? But he'd had to have had more than two sleeps in his lean-to. No matter, he had done that. That may be why Kavita had pushed him to leave so badly. And why Neil was always so jealous of him. What Neil would do with Anand's growing powers would never involve birth from the earth. Unless it resulted in something for him to take.

At first, watching the little fiddleheads poke up from the ground had simply been Anand's main source of entertainment. However many nights it had been, he had watched them, staring from the safety of his shelter. Some of the structure had been left there from someone before, and some of it he had added on to, leaving something for the next person who may need a place to stay, leaving behind something better as proof he had been there. A sign that he had made it and had left.

It was the morning after his first sleep in the lean-to that Anand realized that it was his power that was making the ferns grow. He had willed them to expand and grow, simply by using his thoughts, focusing his energy towards the plants making their way out of the forest floor. He had watched as the pinecones that rested on the earth like matte brown gems stayed still while the moss and scattered pine needles parted to allow for the fern's delivery. Anand had watched as one fern lifted a dead leaf towards the sky as it emerged and felt time return to its regular tempo after the leaf flew away on a gale. Once Anand knew he held the power to do that, he accepted that he held a responsibility to learn what else he could control.

A long time ago, when Anand was much younger, maybe 10 years back, there had been a teacher's day at school. With classes canceled for the day, his older sister Kavita had gotten permission from their father to take her little brother to the botanical gardens. They had ridden two buses to get there and when she saw Anand was fascinated by the shape of the furled fronds, Kavita taught him that they were called fiddleheads. Together they read the signage throughout the fern room. Anand learned not to eat the fiddleheads (*they are carcinogenic, chotu, they cause cancer*) and that ferns could be used to brew beer. He remembered learning about the ferns while obsessing over the fiddleheads. How perfect they were, to spiral upon themselves, so teeny, and then slowly rocking the surface above them, back and forth until the fronds began to bulge, swelling until they burst out of the earth. A video played and Anand was mesmerized by the force of the spirals, so strong, the plant swaying back and forth under its own effort in order to grow tall and reach up out of the earth, to make it in the competition of life on the forest floor. Anand had wanted to feel one of each species, but the staff enforced a 'no touching' policy. He remembered as though it had just happened, the heat he felt in his face after he had embarrassed Kavita by asking the lady standing at the door for permission. The staff member scolded him "no" and then watched the two of them as they took their self-guided tour, making sure they knew she did not trust them to be alone with the ferns.

Anand had been bewitched by them as he stayed in his lean-to; how strong they must be to break out beneath the weighted blanket that covered the earth. Anand had known that birds have beaks that help them break out of their eggshells, but he had not seen anything that birthed itself in real life before the ferns he helped grow. Why would he have? He'd seen the trees bud each spring, along with the signs of new life from their robin neighbors, the broken teal eggshells standing out against all the natural colors he saw. And baby bunnies, of course. But he had never seen anything like what he had witnessed the past few days, something trying so violently to be seen, to be made, to exist. His father wanted him to focus on school and his instrument, no time to wonder-dunder. Anand had been assigned the drums as that had been his father's dream for himself, orchestra *and* marching band would look good on his college applications. He may even get a few scholarships.

Anand had been wondering a lot lately. There wasn't much else to do. Although it may not have been his choice of instrument, Anand did always see himself as a percussionist but after he saw the ferns, he couldn't help but wonder if things would be different for him if he had been a violinist, one of the star pupils in orchestra. First chair violin instead of all the way in the back. Anand made do though, wherever he sat, he had loved finding music anywhere it wanted to be found. Watching the ferns unfurling made him find music within himself. Usually, he just played the music that had been handed to him.  Now that he had witnessed the ferns birth themselves, felt that he had *done that*, it was a good thing he would never be going back to orchestra. He could never look at the violinists in orchestra the same way again. All he would see is that perfect spiral of the instrument, if the spiral helped the sound in any way, how many spirals were there, within that one stringed instrument? It had nothing to do with the person sitting in first chair. Man-made or Bhagwan-made, the spirals he had found would forever tug at him. He would be forever drawn to seek them out wherever he looked.

It had been the Friday before Mother's Day when his only sister had planned that trip for them. Kavita had always been more of a mother than a sister to him. She always looked out for everyone else first. Even though she had expressed no desire to be a mother, she treated everyone as though she was their parent. It suddenly struck Anand that he couldn't remember the last time he had even thought about his big sister. Kavita had stayed with their brother so that Anand could escape. He had been hiding in his lean-to for too long, so long he had forgotten about her. All the hiking had really tired him out. He had walked for hours, barely taking rest. He was not used to it, and it took quite a bit of concentration, making sure that he stayed undetected while also not injuring himself. Slipping on a mossy rock, getting turned around, stepping in a puddle and ending up with wet feet, tripping over a log, and more had already happened. It was no wonder he was ravenous.

He had been rationing the food Kavita had packed for him but when he woke up after that first day of missteps, he could not help it. He had tried and still ended up hungry. She had instructed him to find the women's bunker. Their compound was only a three-day hike, and he told himself he could go without food. He had plenty of water in reserves in order to finish his travels and find the women who would help him, help her. All he had to do was make it there, they would do the rest, Kavita had promised. They would help Anand's family get out of the trouble Neil had gotten them into. Anand realized he had never said thank you to her for staying   with Gayatri so that he could go. She could have left a long time ago but stayed for Anand and now was doing it once more. The siblings both hated it so much at home, but Anand hated the idea of leaving Kavita home alone almost as much as having to stay there with Neil in charge.  So, he had left in anguish, blaming her, livid that his big sister could just send him out on his own, consumed with the thought of her alone with Neil's cronies, that Anand was just expected to listen to Kavita's instructions while she stayed and didn't have to do anything at all.

Anand turned onto his side and curled into himself. He didn't care that the ground was still damp, it seemed like it was always about to start raining but nothing ever fell, that he was just enveloped by an endless mist. The heavens reaching towards the earth, sensing he needed them. Maybe he was creating that perpetual haze as well; grey days would follow Anand wherever he went as long as he kept this cloudy mood of grief and rejection. How could he possibly feel anything else right now?

He used his forearm as a pillow and breathed in his own scent, trying to find any familiar pull to remind him of home. His new powers heightened his sense of smell and he no longer smelled the familiar aromas of Kavita's soaps or her cooking. Any fragrance that remained could no longer make it to the surface for him, his attempt to inhale comfort was a failure, anything he could smell had been mixed with the farinaceous odors peppered into the forest carpet he had been crawling in. A great contrast to the musty smell of the lean-to; so strong he almost tasted it well after he left the once abandoned structure. It had been filled with mice and birds who had been living there when he first moved in. Anand knew they had sensed his growing powers so took their leave, afraid of what he could do to them as long as he resided in their home. They were right to be frightened, he didn't ask for permission to stay there or wait for their invitation. He just entered and took over their home. Anand began to cry as his 17-year-old body mirrored the shape of the fiddleheads he had been controlling. He doubted the options Kavita had offered him; stay with her and cave under Neil's pressure to join him and his friends, or leave while he could, to find the people who would help them, *if* they would be willing to work without payment.

But Anand did not know why they would help. What if they were like the woman at the botanical garden? Pretending they were there to help but only protecting what they were being paid to protect? Even if Kavita was right and they were willing to help him, to help them, the women wouldn't be interested in giving aid once they learned about his growing powers, that he had no idea how to control.

Would Kavita want him to stay safe and hidden or be brave and unfurl? She herself had opted to stay hidden, Anand had watched her do that time and time again for him. Anand knew that it had always been to keep peace at home. Her disagreement was always silent, so silent it was accepting of the circumstances she was in. "It is easier not to argue with Neil," Kavita had always said, "I choose peace." Anand pulled his knees closer to his chest and began to sob.

If Kavita wanted peace, why did she think he was worth saving?

# Chapter Two

Rashmi felt she deserved a reward but knew no such thing existed. Being alive was the reward. At least that's what she had been telling herself lately. Correction. For an exceedingly long time now. Things had been getting worse and looking back it felt so fast but also so slow. For most of her life she had had it pretty damn good.

In her late teens she had told herself to suck it up because that was just the way things were. She learned that trick from her mother, Anjali, who had bent the truth when trying to get Rashmi into a new school district after Anjali's husband Gopal's death forced them to downsize and relocate to a new area. Anjali had said her daughter was advanced for her age. And yet Anjali always stressed that Rashmi should tell the truth. But out of that very same mouth Rashmi had witnessed so many lies. It was usually motivated by money, a discount at the movies or a better price on an item once they were up at the cash register. In this case her lie was to give Rashmi a reputation of an advanced learner. Anjali was smart, she had planned a great benefit of cost savings as tuition had been exponentially increasing every year since she and Gopal had immigrated to the States.

When Rashmi was the only person in her grade who could not take driving lessons, she challenged her mother about how she happened to select her truths. Anjali justified it to her daughter right away, ready with a reply about how it *was* the truth that Rashmi was advanced for her age. At age 11 she dealt with the death of her father and moving to a new school. She was the daughter of immigrants, directly descended from people who had lived under the rule of the British and survived. Rashmi and Anjali were both advanced, Anjali had told her, all immigrants were, moving to a place where they knew no one and were automatically coded as outsiders based on their accents and features. Anjali had refused to argue with her daughter. Why would she? Rashmi could not see the big picture, focusing on one individual tree instead of the forest, all she wanted to argue about with her mother was that she had been forced to attend an entire summer of what Anjali had nicknamed IILS, Intensive Indian Learning School. Anjali thought that by now Rashmi should be over it.

Why would Rashmi pick a fight with her mother over something she had done years ago? That summer after Gopal's sudden death, Anjali had gone to the library and got all the necessary study materials to make sure that Rashmi would be able to pass the educational standards for 6th grade so that she could begin 7th grade at her new school. During the longest days of the year, if Rashmi started to open her mouth to complain about spending her summer needlessly studying instead of exploring her new neighborhood on her bicycle, or reading for fun before studying for her upcoming exam, Anjali would remind her daughter that for her cousins in India, school was *just* examinations; they didn't have creative writing, life drawing, photography, square dancing, or roller skating. Did Rashmi still want to complain about having to study to take *one* exam?

"What difference does starting a new school and a new grade matter to you now, beti? We didn't know anyone here, who was going to take you to visit your old friends to play? Me? How else would you spend your summer? Sleeping or in front of the TV. Either way, 6th grade, 7th grade, you were going to be at a new school," Anjali had retorted to Rashmi's complaint about driver's education. "It is years later, and you don't have a driver's license, but you are graduating early and will have one more year of income compared to everyone else your age. A head start is all I gave you and you argue with me! Fight, fight, fight. Instead, try to be grateful. Maybe not today but I will wait. One day you will thank me."

Anjali was right. Years later Rashmi did thank her mother. Anjali though, barely acknowledging or accepting the gratitude, her response was a simple shake of her head, her once all black plait now salt and peppered from working non-stop to be one step ahead of any possible situation. Rashmi waited for acknowledgement while watching, the cord waving back and forth as her mother's head tilted in neither agreement nor disagreement. Anjali would insist that Rashmi would have done the same for her, were the tables turned. Rashmi didn't know if that was true. Anjali had made many wise decisions for her daughter and Rashmi was intelligent enough to admit that many of them were choices that Rashmi would never have made. Such as the one that allowed Rashmi to graduate early as a 17-year-old woman and move hundreds of miles away where she argued with anti-choice, anti-woman, anti-progress fanatics outside her university residence hall. She was opposing people who either had no job or school of their own to attend, or as Rashmi thought was most likely the case, whose hobby was shaming the girls assigned to Rashmi's dorm for living in the co-ed dorm they had been assigned to at a public university. Confronting adults twice her age, with signs painted with clever phrases such as *'Sluts live here'* and *'These girls deserve what they get for tempting our sons'*, Rashmi would casually ask these 'protestors' if they took the same amount of time to talk to their sons about moving somewhere sluts didn't live. Sometimes Rashmi would insult them in a way she had learned from her mother, going after a single person and working in a backhanded compliment that they wouldn't decipher until she was well inside the safety of the locked dorm:

"Good for you, getting a university education however you can, no one will know it was standing in a parking lot when you tell them you attended here," she'd smirk. Or "You're so brave to protest women for going to a school you wish you could get accepted into, you stay strong!" And her favorite, "Thank goodness you're still here! I was giving my friends directions and told them to look for the building with all the idiot losers protesting! You are the best, serving as a human landmark *and* I always feel so much smarter walking past you. You make a difference." Rashmi's youthful innocence had given her the perfect armor for her sarcasm, sharp as the blade of Durga's sword.

Whenever Rashmi recollected her days living in Mulberry Hall, she could not help but think about Margot. Margot was on her mind many of these days. Their friendship had been surface level at first, exchanging pleasantries as their daily routines overlapped as was bound to happen with their rooms across the hall from one another. Rashmi still remembered their room numbers after all these years: Rashmi had lived in Room 208, her windows facing Keller Street and Margot resided in Room 209, her windows facing the dining hall patio and garden spaces. They both lacked friends on campus, they each felt isolated navigating independence for their first time. But neither had the confidence to do more than leave their doors ajar in the hopes someone cool would stick their heads in to say hello. Neither made the first move with the other, neither woman seeing themselves as the cool person to do that. It didn't cross the mind of either that someone else would want *them* to pop by for a visit. That someone else would want them to be their friend.

They eventually struck up a friendship based on proximity; as well as their localized neighborhood on the second floor. Their rooms were constantly bombarded by the sound of people taking a shortcut, the slam of the emergency exit door being thrown open as women hurried up and down the stairs, their footsteps and voices echoing back to Room 208 and Room 209. The woosh of women traveling to and from campus using that shortcut was the main topic of their initial floor meeting, after which University Housing Administration insisted the residence advisors hang signs to remind the women that if they chose to be irresponsible and use that door, there would be consequences.

Meanwhile, the men living on their own side of Mulberry Residence Hall were able to pretend they were bringing the ruckus while in reality they were simply selfish humans, never made to feel that they had to 'grow up' or behave in a way that acknowledged that others existed in this very same world. The first few weeks of their freshman year, Rashmi and Margot were receiving updates multiple times a week instructing women to use the filtered water in the dining hall or to refill their personal water bottle on the men's side of the building because the men they shared Mulberry Hall had been urinating in the women's water fountains. Just as a joke.

10

Right around closing time every Friday morning, Rashmi and Margot would open their doors nearly simultaneously to take the emergency stairs down to meet other residents and Izzy, their residence hall advisor, in their floor's assigned emergency shelter area. Rashmi had assumed it had to be some of the same residents who were urinating in the drinking fountains on the women's side of the building, pulling their other hilarious prank of setting the fire alarms off when they came home from underage drinking at the bars. The alarm would blare so loud there was no way anyone could sleep through it. During a particularly cold 'Thirsty Thursday' fire alarm Rashmi half-joked with Margot about her theory and was taken aback by how seriously Margot took her accusation. Margot had her own theory; that it was a competing group of friends who lived on the men's side of the dorm trying to one-up the men who used the women's drinking fountains as urinals. Margot didn't plan to do anything about either theory, but Rashmi reflected on how she felt so much less alone knowing someone else agreed with her about these disturbances being just that, disturbing. University Housing Administrators chalked it up to 'boys will be boys' behavior when the residence advisors complained, trying to make the administrators to see that it impacted the health and safety of *all* residents of the dorm, it wasn't just the girls complaining or not wanting the boys to 'have fun'. Izzy reported back as much during a floor meeting and Rashmi learned that many of the women residing in Mulberry Hall felt hopeless; they were paying as much to attend the University as the men but were left feeling as though they received a tenth of the support from the institution they all belonged to. Margot had asked if any of the residence advisors for the men's floors had spoken to the administrators with the women who went; the silence spoke volumes. Rashmi knew from how Izzy clenched her jaw and stuffed her fists into her hoodie that the resident advisors for the men's side of Mulberry Hall did not care that it was a handful of their own residents making the entire residence hall inhabitable. They probably thought it was hilarious and nothing could be done about a few men "just joking around". Izzy and her fellow advisors were encouraged to learn how to laugh and relax and not take life so seriously but their counterparts on the other side of the residence hall were not given a lecture on how to look to the women as role models on how to behave as representatives of the school in order to create a sense of community for the residents how the women had been trying to do. University Housing had told the women that this was the college experience these young men had been waiting for and there wasn't much that anyone could do about it. "You'll look back on this and laugh, you'll see," one of the administrators had told advisors, all women who were also students, much younger than them, put in charge of enforcing the rules to keep the dorm's residents safe. The women RAs understood the instructions they had been given, boys will be boys and if the girls wanted to be here with them, they needed to adjust accordingly.

One Friday, it had been a cool fall afternoon Rashmi remembered, she was returning back to Mulberry Residence Hall after a particularly difficult Chemistry discussion section where a young man in her class had completely taken over the lesson plan because he disagreed with how the Teaching Assistant enforced the syllabus. Nearly the entire hour had been wasted by him trying to convince the Teaching Assistant to let him turn in his lab work late because it was a football weekend, and he had a math exam on Monday and would not be able to study for the exam and complete his assignment on time. As hard as she tried, the Teaching Assistant was taken off subject again and again by his muttering and attempts to get the other students to complain along with him. When Rashmi saw the entrance to her dorm lined with a larger than usual crowd of parents, alumni, and neighboring citizens once again protesting the University's only co-ed dormitory, she realized that there were so many protestors *because* it was a football weekend.

Rashmi saw signs reading *Coed dorms aren't FOR women's rights, they are AGAINST men's rights* and *Men deserve freedom from temptation* and of course, *Protect men from women who are only here for a MRS degree.* Rashmi had been feeling depleted seeing the crowd as she neared Keller Street. She completely lost her patience when she got closer and began to hear the crowd chanting, "Hey hey, ho ho, these temptress sluts have got to go."

As she neared the entrance to her new home, Rashmi saw Margot approaching and quickened her pace in order to meet up with her friend. Margot was relieved to not have to deal with the crowd solo and told Rashmi as much, shouting a greeting as they made their way through the crowd. As the double doors began to close behind them, Margot turned on her heel to stick her head out one of the doors in order to yell, "Y'alls SONS are the hoes, tell them the next time they skip class it should be to study for their STD test!" The crowd started screaming at them as Rashmi and Margot rushed to get their keys through the second set of double doors.

The two were laughing hysterically as they climbed the stairs to their rooms on the second floor. "I have an idea!" Rashmi declared, high off the chaos.

Margot unlocked her door to throw her belongings into her room and rejoined Rashmi in Room 208. Rashmi threw a blank tape into her cassette recorder and began to squeal, sigh, and grunt.

"What are you doing?" Margot asked in shock, "The door is totally open."

"I thought we should give our fans an idea of what could be happening in these dorms with their favorite sons on campus."

Margot thought about it briefly and then joined Rashmi in making a chorus of sex sounds. It didn't take long before Izzy cautiously snuck a look in through Rashmi's open door to find out the source of the rubadub-hubub and was relieved to see it was just the two women leaning over Rashmi's makeshift coffee table, acting out sounds into the cassette tape, trying their hardest not to look at each other and burst into laughter. Rashmi hit pause once she saw Izzy standing in the doorway, silently judging. Izzy spoke first, "Do you ladies care to

13

explain?" Rashmi shared her plan with Izzy as Margot smiled proudly beside her.

"I love it, and I am here to help," Izzy immediately replied.

The three young women spent the afternoon recording their very early custom version of a 'Sounds of Sex' cassette tape. Rashmi promised them they could pick up their copies very soon. Izzy instructed Rashmi to increase the number of copies from two to ten and promised them she would come back that evening with extra blank tapes. Margot and Rashmi hung out in Room 208 that night, joyfully planning distribution of the tapes. Margot and Rashmi held onto their recordings and Izzy took the remaining copies with her, promising them they would be distributed only to honorable and well trusted revolutionaries.

Izzy delivered on her promise. The following day when the protestors against women's education showed up to Mulberry Hall, they were met with twelve dorm rooms blasting 'Sounds of Sex' into the courtyard and onto the street. And the day after that, Rashmi and Margot had learned six more tapes had been created. On the third day, the entire second and third floors of the women's side of Mulberry Hall were blasting 'Sounds of Sex' from their open windows, most of the women were studying in robes and under blankets but all agreed the cold was worth the misogynists being drowned out.

Within a week the protestors were told by University Housing Administration that they could no longer congregate outside of the residence hall to 'show their support for the men of Mulberry Hall'. Instead, they were relocated to a parking lot far from the heart of campus. Izzy told Rashmi and Margot that the women's residence advisors were asked to stop their residents from behaving in such an unprofessional and vulgar manner and the resident assistants had told the administrators that 'girls would be girls' and that the women in this dorm had been waiting a long time and had paid a lot of money for a college experience like this. The only solution that University Housing could come up with was issuing the anti-education protestors a permit with an updated free-speech zone location.

While Margot and Rashmi had gotten dozens of laughs recounting the story to others over the years it wasn't really that humorous; the entire experience had been absurd, not amusing. What a waste of their time. Why had they chosen to stay in a place where men were allowed to treat women that way? Rashmi was glad she had met Margot and made the friends and connections she had thanks to Mulberry Hall, but she didn't believe it had to be as painful as it had been. She had only been 17.

Rashmi missed Margot so much. No one in The Ladoo Crew could compare and Rashmi was incredibly grateful for the friendships she currently had but could not help but reminisce fondly about her first friend crush. Margot was so cool and confident in a way that was so different than Rashmi. Wanting something like that now, at a time when she had never felt more alone. Their friendship was unique to who they had been and how they had helped one another grow ever since the day Rashmi pointed out her theory that the men pissing in their bubblers were most likely incredibly good friends with the men preventing them from being able to sleep every single Thirsty Thursday.

Rashmi fantasized like she had once done as a little kid, wishing she could talk about everything happening with Margot, knowing that her wish would never come true. She knew that magic and wishes weren't real. Guru Geena's 'no mobile devices' policy meant that while you were living at The LCC (The Ladoo Crew Compound) you were never to reach out to anyone besides The Ladoo Crew for help. For Rashmi this meant never knowing if Margot needed Rashmi or The Ladoo Crew's help. Long ago Rashmi had learned to file away any thoughts of friends reaching out to her only to find out she never received their messages.

"Let those thoughts float away, like leaves on a river," Guru Geena always advised.

Her trick almost always worked for Rashmi. But Margot and her wife Eleanor had been trying to leave prior to Slater Corporation CEO Leonard Steel's announcement to run for Governor in order to overturn 'gay' marriage, keep immigrants out, and run this state like a business. Rashmi had accepted that she may not know where her best friend was for months; she was on the same page as Guru Geena when it came to location tracking devices while at The LCC. Most of the other women in The LCC couldn't wait for their stay to be over so that they could retrieve their devices, wherever Guru Geena had hidden them. Many of the women talked about their phones every day, imagining the likes and messages they were missing, expecting to be caught up on all the latest memes soon after their phones were back in their possession. They just couldn't wait for their time to be up.

Rashmi felt morally superior; she thought she knew best and there was nothing anyone could do to convince her to ever use a Slater Corporation smartphone, smartspeaker, security doorbell, garage door opener with motion sensing light to help neighborhoods be safer, automatic pet feeder, or any other Slater Corporation product. Guru Geena had convinced Rashmi thoroughly many years ago; Slater devices all required agreements that any information collected would belong to the Slater Corporation and handed over to federal authorities, local police, or governmental authorities upon request. In exchange, these agencies were given free Slater Corporation computers, smart devices, tracking devices, opportunities to pilot private surveillance apps, social media groups, and more.

Guru Geena did not need to lecture Rashmi on who made up the staff of the police and local governmental authorities and how they worked in tandem to prevent accountability when they abused their power, harming communities as they violated the oaths they once took to serve and to protect. It was that semester that Margot and Rashmi drowned out the misogynistic protestors that Rashmi had been volunteering at the University's Rape Crisis Center, where she learned that domestic violence was up to four times more common in families with police officers than American families in general. The following semester Rashmi learned about the deep ties in America's history linking policing to racism with many recent documented cases of officers being involved with violent, racist militias and straight up white supremacist terrorist groups. Anjali had raised Rashmi to avoid the police whenever possible and Rashmi had listened to her mother, but it was only once she was much older that Rashmi understood why.

Sometimes it felt as though things had gotten much worse since Rashmi thought she had learned so much about the world, decades ago. Rashmi had to rely on the progress she had witnessed to keep up hope. What The Ladoo Crew was doing would save some but not all; there was a steep price tag for their services. Sometimes Rashmi felt guilty, but she wasn't quite sure why. It wasn't as though The Ladoo Crew was participating in extortion. Everyone had to make a living somehow, and Guru Geena's services were worth every penny. Rashmi genuinely believed that. Together they were building a refuge and unfortunately there were only so many seats on this ride; admission could not be free.

Rashmi tried not to do what she had done most of the time, what she always relied on. It was a dependable way to feel better, a way to stop her from acting on what was most needed to change her own world. Telling herself to shut up with her personal complaints. That everyone knew things were worse for women almost anywhere else in the world. To focus on her own problems in the States was selfish when there was worse suffering everywhere else. She'd grown up in the lap of luxury compared to most women in the world, Anjali had been sure Rashmi knew that. Girls nowadays were facing not being able to go to primary school with men like Steel, Knight, and even Rebecca's grandfather Voss, rising to the top of political power structures. The riches that a few families held were shaping the lives of almost everyone across the globe. Who was she to complain about a damn thing when those three men were trying to make things better for her? It had been an expectation for Rashmi to be educated and now as an adult all Anjali had wanted for her daughter was to have a good job, her own bank account, and her own address. Rashmi held all three because of the

17

generosity of all the men who ruled before. Didn't she realize how lucky she had it?

"Focus on that instead of what you don't have," Rashmi told herself as she laced up her shoes and readied herself to direct the others in that morning's drills.

# Chapter Three

Kavita knew it was time to sit at the kitchen table, chopping onions as she normally did at this time of day. Her father Rohit had always wanted dinner ready right on time, and she had always wanted to honor his legacy in some way so had chosen this detail. As she dug through the wood bin full of onions, she wondered what would happen if that night when Neil came home dinner wasn't ready. No one had asked for this tradition, it was more that Kavita felt that this was her duty, that she owed it to her father for all he had done for her. For his family. Even if she hadn't particularly liked him when he was around. It didn't matter, she would still have dinner ready on time because she knew that if she did not, his memory would one day be erased because there would be no one else left to honor him. Anand had 'run away' last week and Neil continued to pretend that Rohit had never even existed. Kavita sighed with sadness, knowing that this was the only way she would be able to keep her family that remained together, by eating this one meal at their kitchen table. Every day.

It was better when Neil had partial custody of his girls, it felt like family dinner then. On nights they slept over Kavita insisted everyone, be at their assigned seat, ready for dinner, no excuses. There were several other rules of their father's that she followed less closely, she asked that everyone only take what they would eat but she never made anyone stay up with their plate until all the food was gone. On occasion she had observed some of Neil's friends, or as she considered and nicknamed them, the leeches, overfill their plates, taking what she considered more than their fair share. As long as the children had enough, and she always made sure their plates were filled first, there was no reason to say a word to Neil about the leeches continual presence on their land. It would only cause a fight and then she would know even less than she already did about him and his stupid 'friends'.

The hell that their father had put Neil through made mealtimes difficult to begin with and now Neil did everything to avoid the kitchen, grabbing the thermos of chai Kavita left for him on the front porch each morning, and eating at Nick's Club for every meal he could. Rohit and Neil, the two most stubborn men having a stubborn-off is what had caused all this avoidance of eating together as a family. Neil was missing an opportunity to get to know his own daughters because he was obsessed with avoiding his past.

Growing up Rohit had insisted his children waste nothing and know the importance of spending each meal together as a family. His intention may have been admirable, but the time was used focusing on all that Neil had to do to catch up with the other boys his age. Kavita always thought about the time that Neil had taken too much aloo gobi and could not finish it. She must have been about nine, still too young to speak up to her father. Neil was 13, the perfect age to sass his father. Rohit had made his eldest son stay up all night with his plate of aloo gobi, not allowing him to go to bed until his plate was completely clean. Neil refused and so father and son sat up all night at the kitchen table until the sun rose, when Rohit sent Kavita and Neil off to school, never once thanking Kavita for making everyone breakfast (which was obviously not offered to Neil) or caring for her little brother Anand all night.

Kavita had been so worried about young Anand being left alone with Rohit all day. She couldn't wait until next year when he would be in school all day, every day like them. At that time Anand only went to their school for two and half days a week. On the other days he stayed at home with their father. Kavita was certain that Rohit just placed him in front of the television all day while he made his business calls. That day at school Kavita couldn't stop thinking about how Anand must have been punished by their father for Neil's obstinance. Without Kavita there to help keep Rohit's peace, no one would stop Rohit taking his anger out on his kids. Kavita knew that it was rare that he was happy but if he was, he shared that happiness with associates, small chitchat before they got to business over the phone. Rohit never shared any joy with his children. He had never said it out loud, but she knew he blamed them for their mother leaving, taking all his joy with her when she left in the middle of the day without even leaving a note.

Teachers rarely called on Kavita, she always had her work done on time and correctly, so they used their time to focus on students who needed their help more. No adult noticed how distracted Kavita was from learning that day, worrying over Anand being left alone with Rohit's anger towards Neil, who had thought he had won, bragging to his friends on the bus about how he had schooled his dad. At the end of the day Kavita watched Neil nod off on the bus ride home, sleeping with ease in a sun beam while she had tossed and turned all night, trying to come up with a solution to make both Neil and Rohit happy, fretting over ways that Anand might not be left alone with his own father all day. She never came up with one, but she never stopped thinking of how she could help them love one another. How she, a nine-year-old girl could solve all of their problems.

Theirs was never a happy home so Kavita felt unease when all was calm when she and Neil arrived home after the end of their school day. The two siblings walked back from the bus stop together to find their dad had been waiting for them on the porch. Smiling, Rohit announced that Kavita was in charge while he ran errands and ignored Neil as he moved to enter their home. A few hours later Rohit returned with two pizzas, garlic breadstick knots, and a salad with kalamata olives and feta cheese, all from their favorite pizza place, Pal's Pizza.

Rohit directed Kavita to run to the garage to get a can of soda for each of them while he broke up ice in the deep freeze for their glasses. All of the children were excited as this was a true treat, their father always kept soda to himself, offering two of his three kids a sip if he was feeling generous. Otherwise, it was always water or dudh in the morning. Rohit scolded them before they even asked, telling them he wasn't going to waste his money on filling any of their cavities.

Kavita had already set the table and returned to fill their glasses and saw that everyone had empty plates except for Neil. Rohit had replaced the empty plate Kavita had set down just a few minutes before to enact the plan he had been waiting for all day. Their father had wrapped Neil's plate up that morning as his son walked up the steps of the bus, confident he had beaten his father in their family's 'don't waste food' game. So now Neil had to eat cold and stale aloo gobi before enjoying the exquisite cuisine that the rest of the family would enjoy. Rohit was so stingy about spending money on eating out when Kavita could cook for free. There was no way for Kavita to enjoy this treat. Rohit was acting, pretending they were having a fun time, a normal American family enjoying a pizza night together, but Kavita could feel his anger towards Neil with every question he asked about her day at school. Rohit wasn't interested in getting to know his daughter, he was interested in making Neil jealous of the attention he was giving her. Just what he did when he would offer her a small sip of his soda while Neil watched, never receiving that same offer from Rohit to try the forbidden and refreshing soft drink.

But Neil did not care. It had been too many years of being treated as though his father despised him. He did not like his father and did not want Rohit's attention. The one time they were able to have pizza for dinner and Rohit had intentionally made it so that Neil wouldn't be able to enjoy the meal. Neil couldn't touch a slice of Pal's Pizza without first finishing off his aloo gobi. Rohit had filled Neil's glass up with water, he could not even have a sip of the ice-cold soda Kavita was so excited to pour until he gave in to Rohit's intimidation. Which he eventually did. Neil sat at the table ignoring his plate of aloo gobi until he saw Rohit offer Anand a garlic knot with marinara sauce and proceeded to tickle his youngest son's tummy, telling him what a perfect son he was. Neil then shoveled the remaining aloo gobi Kavita had cooked the night before into his mouth, coughing from trying to swallow such a large amount of food, not bothering to cover his mouth in order to make a scene at the table as pieces flew out. Rohit nodded with approval and then served his eldest son a plate of food, slapping him on the back as he told Neil that he knew he would do the right thing eventually and lecturing Neil that if he had listened the first time, he would not have caused all this suffering to himself. Neil finished the second plate his father had prepared for him silently and their father held it over all of his children's heads for the rest of his days with them. As though they had done something wrong, not him.

After that pizza night, if Kavita ever asked if they could order food or go out because she was too tired to cook and clean up after the boys at home her father would reply, "Never forget how generous your papa is, buying you pizza in order to get you kids to eat your aloo gobi. You can pay me back for buying you pizzas and sodas and clothes and blankets by cooking and cleaning for us. If you are tired that is good, you will get good sleep tonight. A tired daughter is a good daughter, no?"

Kavita was brought back from her reverie to her present task of preparing tonight's dinner when Gayatri, one of Neil's five daughters, tugged on her apron. Another afternoon of chopping onions at the kitchen table while minding Gayatri. Five girls, three ex-girlfriends of Neil's she had to deal with. It was only Gayatri's mother who they did not encounter much. She left soon after Gayatri had been born, she had not wanted to have a baby so young, but Neil was idealistic. Kavita hadn't understood why her brother wanted to have a baby so young, before he was ready to be a father or capable of providing for them. The only answer Kavita could arrive at was because he believed it would make him the dad that he had never had. But Gayatri's mother Sally left Shepherd County before Gayatri had celebrated her first birthday, signing away all of her parental rights to Neil.

Neil's other ex-girlfriends would only drop their daughters off at their place for a playdate or occasionally this family dinner. The two women would hang with Neil's group of friends, smoking and drinking with the leeches in the backyard, putting their arms around the different men in an attempt to make Neil jealous. Kavita understood why, they wanted to make him mad and they didn't have too many options. He didn't even thank the women for bringing his daughters directly to him, he acted as though he could not stand the women who had blessed him with daughters. Recently Kavita had learned that they each had thousands of reasons to be mad at him. She had heard from Alfie that Neil owed them money for child support but would only give his daughters gifts randomly, never the mothers the money that he owed them.

Neil's ex-girlfriends held anger towards Neil, but they didn't entirely prevent him from seeing his daughters. Kavita looked forward to their visits because it meant she got to spend time with her family, even if this meant Neil's exes arriving to inspect her home and taking advantage of Neil's status with his boss Nick, asking for favors that Kavita didn't quite understand. Kavita could not blame the women for trying their best to get what they were owed from Neil and the other leeches. Kavita had accepted her role as on-call nanny as part of her duty. She was able to handle this responsibility more easily lately, resigned to her role of eldest daughter because she knew that the way things were going with the proposed curfews, Neil's leeching girlfriends would not be able to visit on their own much longer. Left up to them, they had been coming by less and less this year anyway. Kavita had heard Neil tell Alfie that with the new curfews, his daughters would be living with him, regardless of what the legal custody agreement said. Women wouldn't be able to leave their homes to travel past dusk, how could his exes possibly take his daughters away from him if they were stuck at home?

Why would Neil want his daughters if he was never home to spend time with the one who lived here, Kavita pondered when she had heard his comment.

Kavita despised her older brother for treating his daughters as his personal property. Yet she also held hope, just as Neil did, that her nieces would stay with her if the travel permits for single women that Steel was campaigning for were enforced. It made no difference to Kavita if this State elected him, she had stopped leaving the house because she had no time to. It wasn't that bad, and it helped her feel safe not having to worry about all the men out there, looking for women to take advantage of. She could avoid almost all of them, even the leeches. Everything she needed was already at home or could be brought to her. Besides, her nieces needed more structure in their lives and if Steel could help her with that, he had her vote. None of their mothers were capable of parenting in Kavita's eyes.

"What is it, beti?" Kavita sighed before remembering she had wanted to be a better elder than those assigned to her growing up. She extended her arms out to hug her favorite niece. Kavita realized Gayatri was the same age Kavita had been at the time of the aloo gobi incident. Had Kavita really run the whole house at this same young age? Gayatri had still never even chopped an onion and Neil would be livid if he found out Kavita had on occasion let her stir pots as dishes cooked on the gas stove.

Gayatri threw herself into Kavita's embrace and Kavita pulled her in tighter. Kavita began to feel shame and guilt wash all over her. She would never want that for Gayatri, to be treated as an adult so young. Was Kavita turning into her father? Jealous of the opportunities she hadn't had? Kavita had to get her mind in check, she had almost missed this opportunity for affection with her favorite niece, the one she considered her mini-me, so responsible and always wanting to help her Aunt Kavita. So, she could be like her when she grew up. And Kavita had almost missed all this mutual admiration because she was stressing herself out, insisting dinner be ready when Neil got home from his work at the club. He was only home for a few hours before he left again with most of the leeches, off to place the little money he earned back at Nick's Club, buying drinks as he talked up that stupid parade with his friends. Kavita never complained when her elder brother left because it would be much worse if he stayed at home. And while the leeches weren't allowed in the house, she preferred it when they were off their land all together.

"Tell me a story," Gayatri demanded.

"You know that I have too many stories," Kavita laughed, "Which one should I tell? You will have to sit and help me with dinner then."

25

Gayatri nodded her head excitedly before shouting with excitement, "I get to use the knife!"

"Hmm, let me think," Kavita said slowly, "Your father will be mad at me if you cut yourself. How about today you watch me chop but I will give you the most important task. I want you to smoosh these whole tomatoes."

Gayatri squealed with excitement as Kavita prepped her with a small bowl, a wooden spoon, and the large pot of cooked tomatoes.

"What kind of story should we share while we play chef?" Kavita asked.

"I want a scary story!"

"Oh, my goodness beti, your father will be mad at me if I scare you too much! Let me think."

Kavita demonstrated how to break up the cooked tomatoes with a wooden spoon while she pulled a story together for her niece, sitting down to begin her tale, telling her niece, "This story was one of your Chaachaa's favorite stories when he was your age.

"Once upon a time there was a Demon named Gada. He was one of the mightiest Demons of his era, terrifying many humans when they witnessed his presence. It was not his intent to harm them that frightened them, but the sheer awareness of his power. As you know beti, we humans are the intermediary, the in-between, of Gods, Goddesses, and Demons. Gods and Goddesses possess all of the great human traits while all the Demons possess all of the corrupt traits. We as mortals possess them all. Throughout our lives we will do good and bad, it is our nature. But we do not have the great power these beings have to create or to destroy this world, this universe. To heal or to cause harm to it all.

"Gada was so scary, he would frighten every human that crossed his path as he did his work to destroy so that life could be created, the deities in charge, completing their duties after he started his work. Destruction is bad, nahi?"

26

Gayatri nodded her head and Kavita smiled down at her, "This was a trick question beti. Remember, we are good and bad. We contain it all. Yes, destruction can be bad. Gada would stir great bodies of water so that new life could thrive, but all the humans could see as they watched his work was that floods were amassing, a drowning that they could do nothing about would soon come their way. Gada burned forests down. All creatures would run screaming from the chaos and death he produced. They never realized that beautiful prairies grew back in place of the forests, allowing them to harvest their favorite foods, or that many of the trees had dropped seeds that would only grow if fire first destroyed their protective shells. The humans always overlooked the greater scale of the production Gada was fashioning. We are only here for but a short time beti. We can't see it all."

Kavita saw Gayatri nod in understanding so continued with a smile, "Of all the traits Gada possessed, the one which everyone overlooked the most was that Gada would do anything which was asked of him. Gada's loyalty knew no bounds. Everything he destroyed was in order to create. Gada trusted that if he was asked to destroy, it must be out of love and loyalty. Gada trusted there was a greater plan that he did not need to see. He only needed to help create motion or momentum for the plan to be enacted.

"Lord Vishnu admired Gada for these traits. Although Gada often created a commotion that was difficult for the humans to handle, if a tiny bird landed on him and asked Gada to bring him to water, Gada would drop his task to help this tiny bird. Knowing this, Lord Vishnu disguised himself and approached Gada one day.

"Gada may or may not have recognized Lord Vishnu. That does not matter. What does matter is that when Lord Vishnu expressed admiration for Gada's commitment to the master plan, Gada listened. Gada stood silently as Lord Vishnu continued, asking Gada to lend him his bones so that he could create the most heroic maces of all time. Gada would continue his work to destroy, helping the Gods and Goddesses do his work so that they could create.

"Gada was pleased with this request and immediately destroyed himself. He used his power to rip himself apart, handing his bones to Lord Vishnu until he could no longer do so on his own. There was no way for Lord Vishnu to express his admiration for Gada's sacrifice and loyalty. And so, as he created the maces, he renamed the weapon Gada. Handing them to his disciples, he made them vow they would honor the name of the weapon, remembering that the Gada is a weapon of loyalty, a commitment to the greater good."

"This story isn't scary at all," Gayatri interjected.

"The story isn't over yet," Kavita laughed, "Keep listening if giving up your bones isn't scary. You know who I do puja for every fall?"

"Durga puja!"

"That's right beti. Tonight, before bed we can go look closely at our Durga tapestry, and when we do, you will see Durga is holding a Gada with one hand."

Gayatri looked at Kavita expectantly so Kavita returned to her story, "Alright beti, we will go look after we finish chopping and smooshing for tomato curry. But when we go, you must examine Durga's Gada. You already know Vishnu needed Durga to slay the Demon named Mahishasura. Now you know why she was given one of the Gadas made from Gada's very own bones. All of the male Gods were unable to defeat Mahishasura, they needed Durga's feminine powers in order to do so. Durga used all of her weapons to defeat Mahishasura and it took nine days to do so. After Mahishasura's defeat, all in the world wanted to thank her for preserving the universe and containing order for all living beings.

"There was a forest, and in this forest lived an incredibly wise black cat named Saaya. Saaya called all the beings of the forest together to ask if they could work together in order to express their gratitude to Durga for preserving the universe and their home. The honeybees were some of those most grateful for Durga's fight to bring order back to the universe, but the Queen Bee, named Shahad, did not want anyone else getting credit for the honeybees' gift to her. Shahad

28

told Saaya thank you but no thank you, that all beings knew that the Gods and Goddesses were drawn to the honeybees' nectar and loved them very much, how could Durga ever thank a cat for a gift of honey when all deities knew honey came from a honeybee?

"Shahad, The Queen Bee, flew away and with laughter buzzing from her belly told this tale to her worker bees and to her drone bees. They felt adored by the Gods and Goddesses having learned their Vedic chants and calls to all across the universe through the shankha were inspired by the honeybees' very own buzzing. The Gods and Goddesses joined the honeybees each day in appreciating one another, the enlightened ones feeling the buzz in their hearts and bones and having their speech sweetened with their honey. Together the bees laughed at Saaya for thinking they would ever allow a cat to take credit for their celebration to the divine.

"Shahad, summoned all of her workers together and told them to work overtime, to create an offering of honey that had never been possible before. A gift that Saaya and the other animals of the forest could never compete with. The workers toiled, gathering all they could to bring back to the hive for the combs. Shahad sacrificed her own status as she knew that new hives were needed in order to deliver the bounty of honey that she desired to show her devotion to Durga. As Shahad's colony became honey bound she accepted her fate and instructed her workers to begin preparing for a new Queen honeybee. She was sad at the idea of no longer being the most important Queen Bee and was repulsed at the idea of having to share power with Queens who knew less than her but accepted it for she knew that the sacrifice would mean much more honey to offer in respect to Durga.

"As Shahad supervised the creation of five new hives, before each swarm, all workers, drones, and each new Queen honeybee was required to commit their hive's loyalty to her. Each Queen was required to admit they were below her and must pay respects up to her, as Shahad was essentially their creator. Shahad repeated her instructions before each swarm flew off, all of the honey created must go to Durga, none was to be used for anything else. The new Queen honeybees did not understand the master plan, but agreed to it, hoping that once their bounty was delivered, they would be free to supervise their hives on their own. Each hoped to live a life where they no longer had to report what they were doing to Shahad.

"When the bounty of honey was ready, Shahad invited Durga to their forest to inspect the honeybees' offering. Shahad was surprised to see Durga arrived on a tiger and a lion had also accompanied her. Shahad knew that Durga rode her tiger when she wanted all to know her power was to protect the universe from evil and that Durga rode her lion when she wanted all to be reminded to keep uncontrolled immoral behaviors in check. It was rare to see Durga with two feline companions so Shahad was worried that Saaya had done something, the cats working together to impress Durga. Shahad hid her concern that Saaya had planned retaliation in response to her refusal to join in on the gift from the forest and greeted Durga with a comment that she must have brought both companions to help carry the large bounty away.

"Durga did not respond, simply replying with a beautiful smile, demonstrating that she was incredibly pleased with the honeybees' teamwork. Durga pointed to Shahad with her Gada, speaking for the first time to say, 'Your offering of honey is an honorable symbol of your loyalty to me and your desire for order in the Universe, just as this Gada gifted to me is a symbol of those same values. I am overjoyed that you would thank me in this way. It was not necessary so I must thank you in return to express my loyalty. Just as Gada would have done, any request you have for me, I will do for you.'

"Shahad was relieved that Durga and her feline companions were not upset at Saaya's side of this tale and was taken aback at Durga's response. The Queen Bee had not expected an offering from such a powerful deity as Durga to such a tiny insect as herself. Shahad thought frantically for what she could request as the felines approached each hive, Durga loading their packs with honeycombs. As Shahad saw Durga was nearly done loading her companions' packs, she still did not have a request for Durga. As she was the most senior Queen honeybee, there was not much else she could possibly ask for.

"Durga finished strapping the packs onto her companions backs and called Shahad over to say her goodbye. Durga offered one last time the opportunity for Shahad to have anything that she requested and without thinking, Shahad blurted out a request, believing it would please Durga and then she would continue to visit Shahad in the forest, cementing her relationship with the Goddess, making sure that Saaya knew he was not the ruler of the forest.

"'Durga Devi, I worship you only. My honey mixed with dudh is an offering that can sustain all. Humans, deities, cats, all living creatures can live off my nectar. I hope you will consider me and any honeybee your attendant. We will exist only to create honey for you. All I ask is that you provide me and all honeybees with a toxic stinger so that if anyone comes after *your* honey nectar, they are poisoned and learn a lesson to never take that which belongs to Durga.'

"Durga's feline companions immediately bristled at Shahad's request. Durga watched as their spines curled and their shapes grew larger as cats do when they begin to feel fearful or insecure in different surroundings. While Durga felt loyalty from Shahad and her team of honeybees, she grew frustrated at Shahad's request. It was because of her love for both Shahad and her feline companions that she chose to partially honor Shahad's request. As Durga spoke, all of honeybees stopped their buzzing in order to listen to her judgement.

"'I shall grant your request but in a different way than Gada may have done. For you to wish harm upon your neighbors in this world in order to worship me is a curse upon yourself. You admit your nectar can nourish all but would poison those who are so desperate they would steal it. You are grateful to me, but you do not see that I fought only to prevent continued suffering in this universe. I thank you for this gift of honey and in return I shall grant your request. I bless you with a stinger to attack anyone who comes to take *your* honey. Do not look so pleased Shahad. Shall any honeybee sting another creature, the attack will be fatal to the honeybee. Choose wisely when to attack with your new stingers, for death will be certain if you wish to protect your nectar from others in this world.'"

"That's it?" Gayatri asked Kavita.

"You didn't think that was scary?" Kavita asked back, surprised.

"No, it would have been scary if Durga and her kitties attacked all the hives, so she could destroy everything with her Gada and her wrath. Destruction was the only scary part of your story."

"Destruction can be scary," Kavita agreed.

# Chapter Four

Anand watched his brother's friends hike across the bridge. First one way, and then back again. Back and forth they marched, on and on. If they could see what he saw, they would stop and turn around, vowing to never step on that bridge ever again. As Anand felt his magical powers growing, he was able to get in touch with more of the magic in this world. Just a short while back (he wasn't sure how long it had been exactly) when he would spy on the men going through their drills, all he noticed was their cadence. How they tried hard to get their steps to match with one another and with a rhythm. Onbeats that pulsed through the blood his father had given him. He watched the leeches struggle to find their pulse as one body and now sent them the cadence from his own blood, commanding them to slow as he relaxed to calm the beat. His magic had grown so strong, simply releasing the tension he held help them begin to march slowly, to hit the beat from where he laid and kept watch.

At first, he thought he simply noticed the bridge moving, wobbling as the men marched, practicing their formation. Today Anand could see trailing movement, lines that showed where the bridge had been and where the bridge was going to go as the men took turns marching back and forth. Sometimes the men left trails as well, moving fast, moving slow. Right now, the bridge was in motion and Anand could see all potential movement the bridge would make given the chance. He had doubted what he saw with his eyes and so conducted two tests. The first was when he watched the bridge when no one was around. He saw no message that the bridge was trying to send him other than it felt at peace, standing still. The second test was when he came back to see what would happen with no vision. Anand stood still and listened to the men marching, even with his eyes closed he felt the magic beating in his blood. He had no sight yet could visualize the images the pedestrian bridge was sending to his brain. He tried again and again. Right then Anand closed his eyes and received the bridge's message, denying himself vision Anand could see all past and future movements as the men marched back and forth across the bridge. There was no other test he could think of. His magic was real and calling for him to watch the movement of the bridge instead of making his way to the compound.

Anand tried blinking to cleanse his vision and still didn't understand what message the bridge was trying to send him. But with his eyes clenched shut or held wide open he did know that he recognized his brother Neil's voice screaming at the men to get in line and act as though they wanted to fight in Nick's militia, to prove that they belonged. Anand was familiar with Neil's command to stop acting like a pussy. Anand tried to calm his heart as he listened to his brother tell the leeches that if they couldn't get their shit together that they weren't worthy enough to march in Nick's Salute to Straights Parade.

# Chapter Five

Rashmi was distracted as she led the women in drills that morning. Her personal practice usually helped ground her so she wasn't so distracted when teaching the basics to newbies, but this morning she couldn't stop thinking about how her own mother, Anjali, had always told her not to complain. *Please just be grateful for every breath beti, otherwise shut up.*

The distraction was all Rebecca's fault because she had never, ever had anyone in her life tell her to shut up. So now all of The Ladoo Crew had to tame her incessant complaining. About the weather. About the birds singing too loud. About the water tasting 'gross'. About her own damn ponytail that Rebecca had styled herself. Rashmi had a hunch that while Rebecca had never been told to shut up before she arrived at The LCC, it wasn't going to be too much longer before she heard it for the first time.

Rebecca had been dropped off at The LCC earlier that week. Guru Geena had given all of The Ladoo Crew ample warning. Rebecca's father was Miles Voss, the son of the third richest man in the world, technology magnate Richard Voss. Rebecca's mother was reality television star Stiffany Reynolds. Stiffany was the daughter of Olympic gold medalist Jonathon Reynolds and rose to fame as a reality star after her father encouraged her to work with coaches and release a sex tape that showed what she was capable of but didn't go *all* the way. Jonathon wanted to make sure Stiffany had a career of her own and thought this would work to increase her chances of getting a deal with Slater Television. Slater Corporation had announced they were starting several new satellite channels, including one targeted for women, to help them reach their best potential as lovers, or for some women, to help them find a lover who would stay with them.

Rashmi knew Stiffany's sex tape was nothing like that cassette tape she had made with Margot and Izzy her freshman year and she was very much ok with that. She didn't mean to come across as judgmental but picked up that she did when she vocalized to Geena Auntie that there was nothing else she needed to learn from Stiffany's sex tape/audition. Rashmi refused to watch it to gain intel on Rebecca, their potential new client. She wasn't the only Ladoo Crew member who left the viewing room, that was as comforting as it would ever get at The LCC.

Rashmi had always been a romantic. She believed it was important to please your lover but not that anyone was inadequate in doing so. It's just that to be a good lover you needed to be able to trust one another. And that took time and commitment. To be good lovers it was of upmost importance that you were able to communicate clearly with one another. To feel satisfied by a lover you had to feel safe with them. Slater Corporation had money to make on romance. On feeling loved. Their executives knew they could make some money by convincing women that men didn't care about that sort of stuff. That men were different. That if you wanted to keep a man, a woman could try a few other things first, and then maybe trust would come. If you watched a little Slater TV, it wouldn't take too long to come across a commercial teaching everyone watching that if women wanted a man to trust them, they had to show their trust first by learning how to give men access to their bodies. That had been one of Stiffany's most memorable promos, a man's hand sprinkling sugar on her slightly open, plumped and glossed lips as she kneeled in front of him. In front of you, the viewer. Slater TV wanted women to know it wasn't that big of a deal to wait; nobody really did that anyways. Why waste time with a game of cat and mouse? The fact that women wanted co-ed dorms decades ago had proven that. *Girl, if you found a man that you want to keep, you need to work that body to keep him!* is what Slater Corporation advertising executives told the nation in promos on billboards, magazines, and anywhere else they could get new viewers. If there was potential revenue, they would obtain it.

Slater TV sold women guidance from men, told by women. They wanted women to know that sex was what men needed to feel close to their wives and/or girlfriends. To be happy at home. To stay at home. To stay with them. Slater Corporation had gambled and won as they literally banked on the insecurities of women, gaining profits for a few individual shareholders by preying on women who lived in a world that thought they were never doing enough to begin with. And if a woman happened to feel some confidence in the bedroom, Slater TV was here to let them know there was a lot that they didn't even know they were bad at. Luckily, Slater TV could fix that for them!

Now, after a generation of kids grew up watching Slater TV, there were plenty of young adults who believed that programmed Slater Corporation values were their own. Rashmi had scoffed at the absurdity of Slater TV propaganda. However, the proof it had been a success was right in front of her eyes.

Whether it was the skills Stiffany displayed on her audition tape or her father's connections as a world-famous Olympic athlete, Jonathon's wish for his daughter to be rich and famous came true. Stiffany rose quickly as the star of *Rub,* Slater TV's channel for women. Soon she was hosting sex competition shows and sex pageants. Gossip magazines began leaking stories of Miles Voss having a very specialized fetish for Stiffany as several girlfriends came out saying as he got sick of them, he would stream old episodes of Stiffany's show *Feel Me* while he spent time with whatever woman he was with. As long as he had access to their bodies, they would keep him, right? Rashmi knew there were more details to those stories, but she didn't want to know, she hated thinking about it at all. Sad wasn't quite the right word.

Slater Corporation saw an opportunity to combine audiences and had a very special episode of *Celebrity Matchmaking* on their family channel. They advertised the special for weeks and the buzz grew as the celebrities stayed on their respective properties in order to avoid speculation about how their date went. No spoilers allowed.

Slater Corporation executives won again, their advertising campaign worked as the anticipation coupled with the desire to see Miles and Stiffany together or apart was driving almost all celebrity storylines. When they announced the special, Slater Corporation didn't care whether Miles and Stiffany hit it off or not. As the gossip magazines spiraled with new conspiracy theories, they realized the potential that had landed in their laps. They gave Slater Corporation gossip magazines the ending they wanted, presenting them with Stiles as their celebrity couple name, while alluding that the date would not work out. Miles was old money, his father or his father or *his* father had basically invented most technology in American homes today. Miles was paving a new path for himself as a philanthropist and polls showed most viewers thought he was too good for Stiffany. She was the daughter of a college dropout who happened to get lucky at the Olympics, and knock up one of his groupies, who died of a drug overdose before Stiffany had a chance to meet her. The rumor was that Stiffany's mother went out to get high the very same night she came home with Stiffany from the hospital. Jonathon found out and vowed to get full custody of his daughter after that, he had no idea who Stiffany was being babysat by. Stiffany gave sex tips while Miles gave away the gift of his fame wherever he was present. There was no way Miles, a descendant of America's founding family would ever work as a partner to Stiffany, the daughter of nobodies. And American viewers told Slater Corporation that they didn't want the couple to succeed.

Once Slater Corporation learned the nation's viewers were rooting for Stiles to fail they saw the opportunity to give their viewers what they wanted, a show starring people they loved to hate. Rashmi was cynical enough to predict this and confirmed it was true as she read over the intel Geena Auntie had provided. Slater Corporation had run the numbers and convinced Miles and Stiffany to hit it off when they went out on their date and sign up for a ten-year contract with Slater TV. Stiffany could hand over hosting of *Feel Me* to a younger host (she was almost 23 after all) and transition to having a new show all about learning to navigate dating a billionaire 40-year-old. Miles was convinced when the executives casually mentioned how good it would be for the causes he cared so much about, they could even give those causes free advertising; a write off for everyone involved. Win-Win-Win.

But a Lose for Rebecca. Season One of *Stiles Nation* was all about Stiffany and Miles learning to deal with one another's quirks as they fell in love. Season Two's storyline was mainly about one half of Stiles telling the other that it was time to move in and the other half freaking out at the idea of committing to living with someone who was basically the opposite of you. Season Three was rebranded as *House of Stiles* and lead to the 'surprise' engagement season finale. On and on it went. Each season a slight rebrand for the viewers at home, so no one was ever bored. There was the season of wedding planning and then season over the fight for Miles' sperm (of course Stiffany was still not good enough for the Voss family after all these seasons, that sperm had been saved for the world's most perfect incubator), followed by a season of *Stiles IVF Trials,* and of course there was the season where Stiffany was pregnant. And a special two-hour episode where they debuted Rebecca Voss on Slater Sunday Night News. There were infinite storylines and after ten years, Stiles signed on again. Rebecca was now old enough to have her own agent and Voss family lawyers considered her Voss property based on the prenup Stiffany had signed. It was about to happen, and the time had come for Rebecca's spin off. A lot of the world had watched Rebecca grow up into the young woman who stood sparring with Norah today. It was because a lot of the world watched young Rebecca grow up that she stood complaining about sparring with Norah today.

It was only last week that Richard Voss, Rebecca's grandfather, had contacted Guru Geena requesting The Ladoo Crew's services. As Guru Geena must have known (she hadn't) his granddaughter would be turning 18 soon after the election. Guru Geena sat in The LCC's workshop with her privacy armor on as she listened to the third richest man in the world tell her that he was afraid for the safety of his granddaughter. Each day the Slater Corporation, Voss family representatives, and Rebecca's parents were getting marriage and virginity proposals on Rebeca's behalf. Richard was worried about Slater Corporation using Rebecca in this way and was requesting refuge for Rebecca at The LCC until he was certain that she would not be taken advantage of by Slater Corporation or her parents any longer. Rebecca's contracts with Steel TV were up for review every 90 days and in just a few days he would be making sure that the contracts never made it to Rebecca or Stiles. Voss asked if Guru Geena would help Rebecca. Guru Geena instructed him to call back in 23 hours, hung up, and buzzed Rashmi in to advise her.

After The Ladoo Crew did the research that needed to be done for the Rebecca situation (they had to keep all their current clients safe after all) they voted and unanimously agreed to take Rebecca in. Everyone knew that it would be a challenge, but no one expected quite how much Rebecca would challenge them to rise to the occasion of protecting her.

Like most guests visiting The LCC, Rebecca did not want to be here. To have to be here without her mobile device, going cold turkey from receiving non-stop adoration and admiration was too much for her. Rashmi didn't mind saying it. Rebecca Voss was a fucking brat.

On her first day Rebecca refused to use a beginner's gada, crying that it was too heavy for her. Johanna had to run out of morning drills to craft Rebecca a child's gada using the cardboard from a roll of paper towels, masking tape, and some balled up newspaper. The beginner gada weighed two pounds which was too heavy for Rebecca, so she stood to the side, refusing to even hold it. She held no interest at all in the gada, even after learning from her grandfather that her body was currently being bid upon and that any woman who took basic training from The Ladoo Crew could easily stop anyone with that same two-pound gada.

It was Rebecca's third day of morning drills and she still insisted on using Johanna's arts and crafts project. If Geena Auntie permitted mean girl behavior, Rashmi knew The Ladoo Crew would all be laughing at her. Rashmi hadn't watched many of the episodes of the

Stiles Franchise but had walked in and out of the room enough while some of the girls were 'doing intel' to see Rebecca regularly worked out with an elite personal trainer. Rebecca was the granddaughter of an Olympic gold medalist and now Rashmi was listening to Rebecca struggle with a simple gada stab drill, complaining to Norah that the gada wasn't long enough to stab anyone with.

Rashmi walked over to Rebecca and Norah and asked Rebecca if she was interested in advice on technique. Rebecca crossed her arms in refusal and was taken off balance when Rashmi demonstrated the stab drill anyway, invading Rebecca's space. As Rebecca regained her footing Rashmi tossed the gada in the air and kept her eyes on Rebecca as Rebecca and Norah watched it flip down. Rashmi caught it with no effort and shoved the handle at Rebecca, offering both an attack and a challenge, "It's usually easier if you shut up. Try again."

# Chapter Six

Kavita looked up at the clock and saw there was plenty of time before she had to have dinner ready for Neil and the leeches. They were like wild animals in so many ways. Kavita considered that Neil may think of them as pets because of how they behaved. When his car pulled into the garage, Kavita could see them all run from the picnic tables he had set up for them, excited to greet their host after hanging out doing next to nothing all day. Outdoor seating for outdoor leeches. He had been talking about building some shelters for them on their land. All Kavita cared about was that they never come into the house.

Kavita asked Gayatri if she wanted to wash and soak the dal and Gayatri nodded her head. Kavita watched Gayatri measure out the scoops and run her hands through the dal, she knew it was the most important job of them all. If anyone bit down on a stone and broke their tooth it would be her fault, but Kavita would pay Neil's price. As they let the dal soak Kavita asked her niece what she wanted to talk about. Gayatri asked if she could go look at Durga now. Kavita smiled as she said, "Of course." The two walked down the narrow but long hallway to the formal sitting room where Durga hung.

Aunt and niece stood admiring the tapestry that had hung in their family's home on two continents. Gayatri pointed at Durga's trident and asked Kavita if Durga's feline friends were afraid to fight in the sea. Kavita laughed as she then motioned for her niece to follow her to the kitchen. Kavita had to keep an ear on all of the house and occasionally mice would run through their kitchen. If their dinner were ruined by mouse droppings, it wouldn't all go to waste, Kavita would still serve it to the leeches, but Neil would figure out what was wrong when the three of them were eating something different. Kavita could not avoid his questioning. He had turned into Rohit. No one wasted food under this roof.

Kavita gestured to Gayatri to sit at the table as she prepared chai for herself and some warm dudh with honey for her dear niece to enjoy.

The day had been another grey one, the leeches would be eating on damp picnic tables, and the idea of a warm beverage with her beloved niece suddenly lifted her mood.

Once their drinks were ready Kavita joined Gayatri at the table and told her niece that it wasn't only fishermen who used tridents. Gayatri looked at her expectantly and Kavita began her next tale, "This is something your grandfather always disliked. We grow up here with European tales of Gods ruling the seas with their tridents. You should know the weapon's real name is the trishula and it was Lord Shiva's weapon before it could belong to another, for everything that exists is because of him, nahi?"

"Destruction," Gayatri agreed.

"Yes, and there is creation and preservation as well. Three occupations for us to take on to make meaningful change. But this is the trishula. Your grandfather taught me that only one who is able to properly balance the three properties of the trishula can wield the weapon. No human can ever hold the weapon for too long, for each human is holding at least one of the three qualities at any time, more than the others. The first blade represents your Tamas, or lazy qualities like right now when I see your eyes getting heavy from these damp grey skies and your warm drink."

Gayatri snapped to attention and Kavita smiled down at her saying, "I am only teasing, you rest, beti. Rest so you can remember what I am teaching you.

"Ok beti, for our quiz later, remember Tamas is when you are feeling lazy, like you can't just get up from the couch, no momentum. Then a blade for Rajas, not a king but like when a king of the jungle, a little kitty cat has a big burst of energy, that is him showing his Rajas, he is feeling full of energy and passion for momentum that he can't stop. And the final blade of the trishula is Sattva, how you feel right after that first bite of our tomato curry and follow it up with a taste of our cucumber raita. You feel at one with the work you've put in, just completely satisfied. At harmony with yourself and with the universe.

43

"Now remember, Lord Shiva gave Durga his trident so that she could defeat Mahishasura, and she was successful partly because she is always able to balance the three qualities in order to wield this weapon; Tamas, Rajas, and Sattva all in equal balance in order to use the weapon's power. It is not only humans who struggle with this balance though, almost no living creature would be able to wield the trishula. If one is able to, it is only for a short time. It is not expected that we could wield all three qualities in balance in order to fight with the trishula in battle. That is why we are in awe of Durga and Shiva. They inspire us to be courageous because of their wisdom and equanimity, while also reminding us that there will rarely be a situation where we will be gifted all three blades.

"Once upon a time, under our very sky, but still somehow a world away, there lived that very smart black cat named Saaya. Saaya was very happy most of the time. Some days they woke up very hungry but happy they were in a warm sunbeam. Other days they woke up very hungry and were drenched from not having enough cover during a big storm. Some days Saaya was the ruler of all the land, no predator could compete with him. Other days humans came into Saaya's land and hunted his neighbors with machines that made loud scary noises and left the other animals screaming in pain. When Saaya was the only hunter, they made sure it was over quickly and as painless as possible and then invited all to join as Saaya dined. The humans waited, wanting to make sure the animal was truly dead. Sometimes placing their fingers on small screens and then handing them to the other humans so they could disgrace the animal, picking them up and smiling with the body still warm in their hands. Saaya had even witnessed the humans coming in to dump bags of food for neighbors to find so that it was easier to kill the animals residing in Saaya's forest. It was more than once that Saaya managed to survive because he often became a shadow to humans, they did not see the black cat so well with their eyes.

"On a day Saaya was feeling low, they thought that they saw their own reflection before realizing they were not at the lake. Saaya felt drawn to approach their own shadow and saw it was definitely not a self-reflection. Saaya was so glad to know they were not going mad. Saaya was a skinny but muscular feline with many scars and some patches of fur missing from their back and chest while this other black cat was plump as could be with thick, luxurious fur. Saaya extended a hello to this new neighbor and asked if they were lost.

"'Oh, dear goodness,' the new cat began, 'My human brought me here with her Papa, but I did not notice when they left. Do you know how to get back to town? My name is Midnight, and I would so ever appreciate your help.'

"'I am Saaya, and I do not help the humans.'

"'But you could help me,' Midnight insisted.

"'And why would *you* help the humans? They set traps to kill us!' Saaya had stopped cleaning their paws in order to properly glare at Midnight with their deep green eyes.

"'I don't know anything about that Saaya,' Midnight continued, 'My good friend, all I know is that I have a lustrous and sleek coat, soft paws, and a full belly thanks to their kind hearts. You however seem to have weight to gain, nails that keep falling out, and a coat that could use a deep wash *and* a good brushing. Perhaps the humans are not all bad, you are living a very satisfying life for all their visits it seems.'

"'Yes, and your belly is full, and your coat is sleek for free? Why is it they care so much about your trimmed nails? What is the cost that they make you pay for a roof that keeps your fur dry?' Saaya asked snidely.

"'I only have to guard their kitchen so that no mice get in the way and steal from them. I would be glad to do that without the free meals. Doesn't that sound much better than the hard work ahead of you? Hunting your own food, finding your own drink, keeping safe from the others, making sure no one else will take your bed. Why do all that work and how can you possibly even keep yourself warm with missing fur and no fat on your bones?' Midnight asked as he walked towards Saaya.

45

"'What's that noise?' Saaya interrupted.

"'Oh that, it's no bother.'

"Saaya inspected Midnight closely and saw he was wearing a collar with a bell. 'And how can *you* possibly hunt anything wearing a bell that announces your presence?' Saaya asked incredulously.

"'Well, you see, I am known about as a rather ferocious hunter, Midnight Meal they call me, I hunt so well in the pitch darkness of night. So, my good friend, Saaya, someone as smart as you will understand it is to keep everyone else safe from me. What if I accidentally hunted the wrong prey? Someone could really get hurt,' Midnight pointed out to Saaya.

"'We are nothing alike,' Saaya announced as they turned and trotted away, 'Please don't follow me. The sound of your bell will announce to all the humans that I am here, and I will no longer be a shadow in the night.'

"'Farewell to you, you raggedy panther,' Midnight called, 'I would rather live like a Maharaj, mota in a warm castle than out here with you.'

"'Farewell to you, Your Laziness,' Saaya called back, 'Your greed makes you believe that you are living in luxury like a Maharaj, but you have none of the independence this raggedy panther has. Good luck finding your humans, start walking and they will listen for your bell!'

"The two black cats walked away from one another, two voids receding, each searching for Sattva, but only Saaya knew that no peace and safety could be held by either while they were running from the terror the humans caused."

Kavita looked at Gayatri for her reaction.

"Humans are the scary story," Gayatri said sleepily.

"*Some* humans are the scary story, beti," Kavita said as she ran her fingers to release the three sections of hair that made up her niece's plaits.

# Part Two

# Chapter Seven

Anand woke up suddenly. Had he even fallen asleep or did his magic just push him forward in time? He looked towards the bridge for clues. The day was still so grey, Anand had never noticed quite how many greys were possible until he had set off on this adventure, but the grey of today, of this moment felt much darker to him than it looked. How could that be? Anand looked down at his hands. There were no trailing images when he wiggled his fingers and danced his hands back and forth. He laughed at the idea of anyone watching him right now. He must look like a madman.

His brother and his friends, the leeches, their militia had departed. Anand could not remember them coming or going. Just the marching, marching, marching. Back and forth across the bridge, above, below, and through the mist. How could he have not noticed them stop? Neil's militia had been playing call and response for so long, and so loud, on repeat:

*Uncle Sam asks you to fight*
*[Uncle Sam asks you to fight]*
*But you need help he ain't in sight*
*[But you need help he ain't in sight]*

*Uncle Sam hands you a shield*
*[Uncle Sam hands you a shield]*
*But Slater Corp hands you Lenny Steel*
*[But Slater Corp hands you Lenny Steel]*

*Uncle Sam wants more and more*
*[Uncle Sam wants more and more]*
*If he asks real nice, he can mop our floors*
*[If he asks real nice, he can mop our floors]*

As Anand tried to sing the call and response on his own, he realized he had no voice. His throat itched with dryness and his tongue felt sticky, like it was taking up too much space in his mouth. All he wanted was to rinse, it tasted so bad all at once, so bad he thought he could smell his tongue. He looked around for the water bottle Kavita had shoved at him along with his backpack as she told him the time had come for him to leave and get help. Find somewhere else to live so he didn't get inducted into Neil's gang. Nick's club. He couldn't find it anywhere. He would have to backtrack to the ferns and then back to the lean-to. He shouldn't have stayed there as long as he had, but his powers had called on him to stay. There was a purpose, but Anand did not know what it was. When he had left this morning, he had told himself to take everything, that he wouldn't be going back to the lean-to by himself. Not until he had made it to the women to come up with a plan to help Kavita and Gayatri. Poor Gayatri would forever be stuck with Neil without Anand's help.

But now he had to go back. Anand was positive he had his things with him when he had crawled to the ferns. Anand finally admitted to himself that he had not wanted to go back there because he was worried his magic was tied to it. That *he* wasn't magic but his stay in the lean-to was making him magic. He had planned to walk straight to the compound, finally following Kavita's instructions. To get somewhere safe to figure out a plan to help her and the girls. Then they'd figure out how to help Neil.

He had wasted so much time, always Papa's favorite but the worst fuck-up of them all. Anand's tongue was growing more uncomfortable in his mouth. If only it would rain. If his magic was real, then it would have right then. Right?

He had to backtrack and find his things. He hadn't eaten in almost a day, without water things could get bad. He wouldn't have to go too far back. Once he had what he needed, he could move forward to help them all.

# Chapter Eight

Rashmi was glad she wasn't supervising on meals rotation this week. They'd had guests who wouldn't eat without an audience and guests who bullied other guests. Rashmi thought about how her mother had described her own childhood; at the age of six helping with cooking, laundry, cleaning, and more while Ladoo Crew guests some of whom were grown adults) needed observation and guidance at mealtimes. It was a comfort to those guests, having The Ladoo Crew wait on them, care for them while they were in this new experience. Rashmi knew that was part of The Ladoo Crew system, to make their guests feel respected so they would listen to their teachers' instructions. It was an easy give, but it really could be exhausting trying to help someone help themselves after watching them have no interest in doing so.

Guru Geena had a very equitable system for LCC duties; each rotation had a good mix of experience to make sure everyone was given a voice when decisions needed to be made and to ensure anyone could fill in for another if or when things 'happened'. She would have to eat lunch with Rebecca Voss next week but for a few more days she was Rebecca-free after morning drills were complete.

Rashmi made her way to the conference room for the mid-morning briefing. Rebecca was likely the main agenda item, but Guru Geena had also mentioned a heightened alert for this weekend's Salute to Straights Parade. There was an unusual buzz in the room, a few of the women were in groups of two or three, hunched over copies of some document.

Rashmi took a seat as Guru Geena tapped her golden gada on the conference room table. "I'll tap twice if I have to," she teased. The women were at attention right away, Rashmi had never seen Guru Geena need a second tap. Maybe Rebecca would break that record, she half-joked to herself.

"Johanna, why don't you get straight to it."

Johanna pursed her lips, a habit that Rashmi noted she would have to gently point out to her, it gave away her nervousness and that meant giving away a weakness. Concealing their vulnerabilities was a skill all worked on as part of The Ladoo Crew Code.

"If you all would pass these along," Johanna started, handing out additional copies of the documents for the few who did not have their own, "What you will find is a summary of a statement given by a staff member who works for the county, within the department of Building Permits. While I know most of you are familiar with our fight against the bridge construction, I think it is important to highlight a few connections between what we've learned from this statement and our previous discussions about the need to build this bridge.

"Over many years Guru Geena has been buying parcels adjacent to The LCC that have any potential to intersect with potential proposed Department of Transportation roadways. One of these included the parcels adjacent to Canary Canyon, where the State ruled against us, stating the county could build the pedestrian footbridge in order to connect our land with the land opposite our side of the canyon.

"The county was not on our side with this case, which had taken many of us by surprise. Guru Geena has been a generous neighbor to the town for decades and the neighbors we do know all agree with us that Shepherd County and the State should not be able to dictate what we do on our private land."

"Which has been paid for in full," Guru Geena interrupted.

Johanna continued as the women in the room nodded in agreement, "No investigation was needed to know that the decision was influenced the moment Leonard Steel publicly declared he was paying for the bridge in order to put a stop to segregation in this county. He all but declared war on the idea of a private security firm run by women in order to protect women.

"The bridge was built soon after the decision was made. We all joked that a bridge built that fast couldn't be safe to walk across but we wouldn't have to worry about it since we would never need to cross that bridge.

"Then last month we learned that AmBackPats, also known as Americans Back Patriots -"

"AMERICAN MEN PAT THEIR OWN BACKS!" Norah interrupted, hollering for laughs and getting some but also a very direct hush from Guru Geena.

Johanna coughed to clear her throat, took a sip of water from the glass in front of her, and then continued with the briefing, "We found out that AmBackPats submitted an application for a Salute to Straights Parade with the Shepherd County Department of Traffic Engineering. The contact's name provided on the application was Nicholas Huber. The application read that there would be 500 participants and that the parade route was to end on the bridge, the purpose of the parade, per the submitted application was 'to highlight the contributions straight males have made to society but never bravely or openly celebrated.' We believe that this application was submitted in order to be approved as an act of intimidation against us by AmBackPats.

"As you can see summarized on the document in front of you, yesterday afternoon Cynthia Lovell from the Department of Building Permits contacted us as she feared for our safety. Cynthia could not come here to give her statement. We were able to speak with her for a short time but what we found out was incredibly disturbing, given Rebecca's arrival to our compound the day before.

"Leonard Steel publicly promised to pay for the Canary Canyon bridge but did not promise to use County approved contractors. Because Slater Corporation was footing the bill, they insisted that they use their own bidding process to find a local construction company. The bid Slater Corp went with belongs to Huber Consultants."

A slight murmur went up even though most everyone had scanned the document and knew this was the buzz about today's briefing.

"Huber Consultants is owned by Nicholas Huber," Johanna continued, "Huber owns some rental properties, several local establishments, sponsors a little league team, and a bowling league. And of course, we are most familiar with Nick's Club, which is a 24-hour diner and in some of the community's opinion, the seedy bar cops are always at; on-duty or off.

"In an effort to save what, a few hundred or thousand bucks, Steel chose someone he could use as an ally in Shepherd County to build the bridge. We must accept the possibility that this bridge was constructed in order to have two access points to The LCC, one of the last remaining security firms Slater Corp hasn't been able to buyout. One access point with a parade of potentially 500 men leading to a riot we would have to deal with so that the other access point is open in order for Slater Corp Security to aid Rebecca Voss' in her 'escape' from our compound. Hiring Huber does not only get Shepherd County men to join in on this parade, but this is an obvious attempt to win votes from the citizens of Shepherd County. We don't know which of our neighbors got a paycheck to build this bridge and what they were told about us when building it.

"Whichever way this weekend's parade goes, it'll result in a great outcome for Slater Corp. Huber shows off Shepherd County's shiny new bridge, that The Ladoo Crew fought against, and how the contract Steel awarded him helped improve his life as Election Day is nearing. Steel will be getting tons of free campaign exposure not just in Shepherd County, but all across the state with this free rally. And it will all be a positive spin for him. It's always positive spin for him because he has the power to spin. Through Cynthia's valiant outreach to us we have learned that Huber has no experience with construction but there has been no coverage on this at all, leading us to believe that no one from the Fanning campaign is aware.

"The construction experience Huber Consultants has under its belt ranges between janitorial services and handyman repair on their own rental properties. We did find that Nicholas had always held an interest in furniture repair and restoration so maybe that counted. But all kidding aside, Huber Consultants has never built a bridge and the one they did build will be transporting 500 men to our land to protest our existence. We must plan for the scenario that they may end up stuck on our side of the bridge. We cannot trust that structure."

The Ladoo Crew said nothing. Johanna met the silence head on. She no longer showed any signs of nerves.

Rashmi met Johanna's eyes and began tapping her gada lightly on the conference table. The other women joined in, the conference table trembling against the floor from the light but rapid taps of the women in unison.

Guru Geena stood up and raised her gada in the air, "For all beings!"

"Azaadi!" The Ladoo Crew called back in response.

# Chapter Nine

Gayatri had run off to gather art supplies, it was her birthday this weekend and Kavita had promised her that they could work on decorations together, she was so excited to celebrate turning ten with her sisters. Kavita so hoped Gayatri's mother would at least send a card, but one hadn't showed up yet. Kavita daydreamed ways she could make Gayatri feel she was special to her, as she washed the dirty dishes that had come along with their prep work. Kavita knew firsthand that there was no one in the world who could fill that particular gap of a mother's love when missing, leaving a very young girl to figure out how to navigate the world without a mother, all on her own. Kavita never wanted Gayatri to think she pitied her, she only ever wanted to help. If she could build a family with Gayatri, she would try to. She'd never be Gayatri's mother but that didn't mean Gayatri would never know love.

Even after slowly washing the dirty dishes Kavita still had a bit of time before she really had to start cooking. Gayatri's fascination with their family's Durga tapestry had made Kavita begin to think it belonged in the kitchen. Her father had always said to keep Durga in rooms that were used less because Durga could be very protective, and they wanted to make sure guests felt welcome when they visited. As Kavita thought about this she realized the kitchen would be the perfect spot for Durga; it was the room where she spent most of her time and would help her feel safe from the leeches.

Kavita felt herself growing angry at the idea of Rohit hiding Durga away on purpose, preventing her from doing her job properly. It was one thing for a woman to correct or scold a guest in her own home, she could understand how that would make a guest feel unwelcome. Almost her entire life she had witnessed men or boys misbehave or react in retaliation after being corrected by their mother, teacher, boss, cashier, barista, classmate, *any* other woman who had no right to speak to them - a man - in that way. But my goodness, what a patriarchal view to have, that Durga Devi could not correct you in *her* own home?

Kavita would make sure that Durga was always in full view so that all of the girls would feel safe when they came over for dinner. If Neil had a problem with it, she'd remind him how he was rarely home and then see what he had to say as he stood in front of Durga.

After she was done hanging the tapestry in the kitchen, she joined Gayatri upstairs and worked to organize everything they'd need to make their home look festive for Gayatri's birthday celebration. She'd be moving from single digits to double, a birthday to remember for sure. Kavita and Gayatri were able to load up all of their supplies and then Kavita sung, "Chalo, I have something new to show you."

Gayatri loved the new kitchen décor, dropping all the art supplies she was holding onto the kitchen table so she could more easily gaze upon Durga. She used both hands to thoroughly examine the tapestry, feeling the beaded and sequined art closely with her fingertips. Kavita hoped that Gayatri's younger sisters would be enamored with the tapestry just as much when they came over for pizza and cake.

As Kavita began the pressure cooker for the dal, she asked Gayatri if she would be interested in learning about Durga's flower, thinking her niece was still young enough to not answer with a 'no'. As she had hoped, Gayatri was enthusiastic about learning more so Kavita leaned against the counter and began, "You see beti, a lotus bloom is one of the most beautiful flowers in all the world. But a lotus flower cannot grow without mud. It is impossible. 'No mud, no lotus' is a famous teaching.

"If you look closely, you will see the lotus bloom that Durga possesses is not in full bloom. It is a symbol of that we are forced to rupture through in order to reach towards the sun and fully unfurl. But once we do bloom, our blossom only lasts so long, it will fall away and decay. It will sink down and become mud, allowing for a new lotus blossom to emerge from the mud."

Gayatri was fidgeting and Kavita encouraged her to play with her art supplies, gathering everything she may need to draw on the big pad of paper Kavita had carried down from upstairs for this very purpose. It was boring to do nothing and Kavita knew that making party decorations was some work, but it was nowhere near the amount of work her own father had made her do when she was Gayatri's young age. Art projects were one thing, but her nieces were all much too young for such responsibility.

Gayatri started drawing lotus flowers on her drawing pad, looking up at the tapestry of Durga and then back down to her pad to follow the artwork in front of her. That her niece felt so inspired by Durga Devi made Kavita's heart swell.

Feeling more confident with Gayatri's previous assent, Kavita continued, "Beti, I have another story about Saaya. Would you allow me to share it?"

Once again Gayatri agreed and Kavita began, "Thank you, beti. You make me feel so important that you want to hear my stories.

"Sometime after Saaya met Midnight, Saaya went to the lake to examine their reflection. There was a clear sky, and the lake was clear as well. Saaya wanted to know what others saw when they looked at them.

"'I don't care what they think,' Saaya said to themselves, peering into the lake.

"As Saaya stared deeper and deeper, they felt a breeze in their whiskers and when they watched them flutter in the lake, they realized they hated their whiskers. Saaya had always had long black whiskers, a prize for birds looking to secure their nests. On this sunny day, it was clear to Saaya that many of their whiskers were now white as Saaya had aged and felt the stress of more and more hunters coming into their forest. Saaya continued looking into the lake and decided that they loved their green eyes the most, they were as green as the meadow got, right before it turned into summer, and all the butterflies were drawn to it, along with Saaya, having fun chasing them as they stalked and bounced through the tall green grasses.

"Saaya stared into the lake for so long, critiquing everything that they saw looking back at them that they did not realize the sun had set and it would soon become night. Saaya tore their gaze away from their reflection just in time for their eyes to cast a reflection back on to a torch a human was carrying.

"'We got something!' Saaya heard the human shout.

"Saaya turned quickly and began to run. Tonight, would not be the night the humans posed holding Saaya's still warm corpse. Saaya vowed to jump right into the lake and dive beneath the surface before that ever happened. Saaya ran and ran but was having trouble seeing in the dark. More now than ever in their old age they had trouble moving at night. But as Saaya ran they realized that their whiskers were aiding their night vision, picking up on breezes so that Saaya knew where to leap and protecting Saaya's eyes from dust as they kicked up the decay on the forest floor, sending it everywhere. Saaya's whiskers alerted them to a small tunnel and Saaya ran down it, their whiskers exactly the perfect length to let them know their shoulders and hips would fit down the tunnel, allowing Saaya to move quickly, safely, and with almost no sound. When Saaya got to the bottom of the tunnel, they met their friend Frank, a fox who sometimes alerted Saaya to the happenings of the forest. Frank invited Saaya to wait out the humans in his den, as long as they stayed quiet, the humans would not be able to find them.

"Frank slept, waiting for the morning to arrive, knowing the humans rarely hunted then but Saaya could not put their mind to rest. All Saaya could think about was how they had thought so little of their whiskers, which had saved them multiple times that night while the body part Saaya admired the most is what had got him in trouble to begin with. Saaya would never go another day without appreciating their whiskers, whatever color they may be."

Kavita looked at Gayatri and asked her niece if she understood what she was trying to say. Gayatri nodded once more, smiling with a pained look in her eyes.

58

# Chapter Ten

Anand had been crawling again, gazing through the forest floor, looking for the glint of the stainless steel that would indicate his water bottle when he found the most perfect stick. He knew it had fallen from an oak. Some of the brown leaves were still attached, still crisp. Anand had been alerted to this fine stick when he slipped, kicking back on the branch as he crawled, one of its leaves crunching under his weight, no sogginess to it at all although there had been so much rain and moisture surrounding Anand and all of the forest lately. Anand held the oak limb in his hand and felt a shudder run through his palms, through his wrists, forcing him to grip the limb tighter. At that, the quake began to run up his arms, through his entire torso, the force so strong it almost caused him to fall on his back from the kneeling seat he had taken.

Anand ripped the smaller branches off the main limb, along with any remaining brittle oak leaves and then pierced the earth with the tool he had made, using all the strength he had to push away. As Anand stood, he knew he had found his magic staff. His wizard's staff.

Anand stood, surveying the land around him. So much green. And so many browns. He still saw all the greys as well. And then a flash of red zipped past in his peripheral vision. When he had been crawling on the earth, he was entranced by the iridescent shells of insects going about their business and the sparkle of minerals in the soil. He had had to stop himself from rolling in the earth, he wanted to cleanse himself with the minerals. He was still so thirsty, but he had wanted to take handfuls of it all and brush his teeth and his tongue, to get as much moisture out of the earth as he could but also so that he could shine with equal iridescence. Cleanse himself with the parts of the earth that were summoning him.

Something had halted him as he held a scoop in his hand, teeth parted, ready to be cleansed. Maybe it had been Kavita looking out for him because he hadn't tried to eat the earth or lick the moisture on the carpet of leaves he crawled through since he shuddered back awake in that moment. He watched the soil drop from his cupped hand to join the forest once again but no matter how much he tried rubbing it off his palms, he still saw it there. He had absorbed the earth. As he stood and assessed his surroundings, he saw light reflect off the stainless steel of his water bottle. He would never have found it if he had not found his wizard's staff first.

Anand began to walk towards the glint in the greens and browns, using his staff for support. He didn't recognize anything here and didn't understand how his water bottle could have ended up in the middle of, well, nothing. As he walked, he began to notice the timbre coming from his wizard's staff as it struck its path.

*Tap. Tunk-tunk. Tap. Tunk-tunk.*

Anand played with the rhythm as he made his way towards his water bottle. A fast tempo. Then slow. He danced with the earth and before he knew it, his staff had taken him to his belongings. Anand threw his arms to the sky, pumping his staff towards the heavens in gratitude. It was not just his water bottle that was here, his black backpack had been set beside it, waiting for him.

He shook the water bottle and decided there was enough for him to take a sip or two. He would have to ration but not as much as if he had had to travel all the way back to the lean-to. If it rained as much as the skies seemed to want it to, he would have enough to drink to be able to find the women Kavita promised would help him.

Anand inspected the remaining contents of his backpack, checking to see if whomever took his things had stolen from him. It looked like most everything Kavita had packed was still there. She had sent him only with his schoolbag so Neil wouldn't notice too much if he happened to see. Anand figured she could have packed his entire room and Neil would have been happy that Anand was gone. Anand packed everything back up into his schoolbag, the hand towels, a second set of clothes, too many pairs of socks (none of which were wool), and underwear all into the big pocket. He sat down and laid his staff on the ground before him and then tapped on it with his maple drum sticks. Feeling no magical message from his wizard's staff, he placed them back in his schoolbag. He was confused how that could be and thought about how Neil would never give Anand money, so he always had to buy the cheapest drumsticks. And keep them safe, hidden from sticky, little hands. There was not much Anand could afford without asking for help and it meant a lot to him that Kavita knew to pack them, even if it was just for sentimental reasons. She was usually just practical; she knew he wouldn't be playing the drums as a runaway.

Inside the large pocket, home to almost every material possession that made Anand who he was, there was another smaller pocket, where Kavita had hidden over a hundred dollars that she had saved up.

"Anand do not spend any of that money unless you absolutely have to. Do not lose it. These women will expect a lot more money than this and all I can do is hope they will see we want to help them even though we can't afford their help," Kavita had said, "You can't come back without them. Once Neil finds out I took from the girls, took from him…"

Anand put the remaining items back inside their home in the midsized outer pocket. Flashlight, scissors, lighter, knife. Anand zipped and then unzipped the outer pocket. He slipped the knife into his pocket and grabbed his wizard's staff. It was time to march.

# Chapter Eleven

Rashmi made her way to check in with Poppy in the workshop, where Rebecca had been spending an hour each day, learning how to tie knots. Ladoo Crew 101. Rashmi had supervised Rebecca briefly yesterday and it was brutal. Rebecca was impatient and grew exasperated when spoken to while she was trying to concentrate. Rashmi had to help Rebecca learn to not blame others when she lost her focus, that when it was a lazy way to fight. It would be difficult. Rebecca somehow managed to have little to no curiosity about asking for help, a peculiarity given that she was in a space to learn to be done once and for all with learning how to tie knots. Rashmi had explained that she only had to learn how to tie the knots once to be given more autonomy at The LCC, but Rebecca just sighed in reply, she was bored of being bored.

Rashmi started at the top, hoping getting the first step checked off would motivate Rebecca to get more checkmarks but she wanted to skip all the basics, telling everyone (no one else had been there besides Rashmi) how stupid it was to learn how to lay a shoelace down properly. And then once she saw how beautiful Rashmi's bow was, she tried to rip up the laminated instruction sheet and jumped up and down on it crying, screaming at Rashmi that she'd never be perfect like her. It only took a few moments of Rashmi soothing her for Rebecca to be in a brand-new mood, never apologizing for her violent outburst but complimenting Rashmi's double Dutch braids to let her know she knew her behavior had been unacceptable. When Rashmi's tried encouraging Rebecca by telling her that if she could braid her own hair into fancy crowns, she could absolutely complete the knots checklist, Rebecca shut down and became uncommunicative. Rashmi hadn't known what else to do so ended the lesson. She wouldn't waste her own time with a student who had no faith in themselves.

There was a reason every guest had to complete The Ladoo Crew 101 knots checklist. If you wanted to play in The Ladoo Room, you had to get your knots down first. Everyone was tasked with creating their own weapon but in order to get that ladoo shape, they had to perfect their mushti knot first. Once it passed Guru Geena's inspection, the student was led to a variety of ropes, to select any fabric or color that called to them to create their monkey's paw weapon. After that they were given a tour of The Ladoo Room, and a seat in the audience. After watching a few matches, they could volunteer as targets and after feeling the impact of running from and being caught by a monkey's paw several times, they could practice throwing on moving targets. Until then, there was space in The Ladoo Room to practice on stationary items or when supervised, outside there was the practice space to allow the student to practice in different elements and under new circumstances.

Guru Geena and Rashmi had discussed Rashmi's lesson plan after the midmorning briefing; Rebecca needed a reality check and together they decided she needed to learn what The Ladoo Crew was capable of. Until then, Rebecca may never have the motivation to learn how to protect herself. In jest Guru Geena had said she was surprised Rebecca had known how to tie her own shoelaces. Rashmi did not tell her that she had thought the same exact thing. Until a few days ago, Rebecca Voss had someone who had dressed her, multiple times a day. That may have been one of the easiest parts of the transition to The LCC for her, a fresh uniform provided to everyone daily.

Rashmi hated that she would be interrupting Poppy during a difficult lesson. Rebecca would see this interruption as a reward for her terrible behavior yesterday. It had to be done though. The Salute to Straights Parade was this weekend, and The Ladoo Crew could not spend most of their resources to protect one client and lose everything they had been working towards. They had to help Rebecca understand why she was here.

Rashmi waved at Poppy with one hand as she approached the two women occupied at the workbench covered with various lengths of string, twine, hemp and nylon ropes. She saw that Rebecca was now

63

working with tying multiple shoelaces, the practice nautical cleat nowhere in sight. Rashmi realized Poppy may have tried to go with something new or maybe she had tried to incentivize Rebecca by handing her the instructions to the fisherman's knot as a more advanced challenge. Once Rebecca got that down, she'd be able to return to the basics and do the cleat hitch much more easily.

There was a definite improvement in Rebecca's mood from just a day earlier when she got frustrated trying to follow along with the cleat hitch instructions given to her by Rashmi. Rashmi had also handed her a board with two long pegs attached to a small length of wood, running somewhat parallel to the board. Rashmi had felt so guilty as she caught herself judging Rebecca for needing another arts and crafts project to learn a basic skill (most of the time the women in The Ladoo Crew easily taught the cleat hitch using the handle on their special stainless-steel mugs) but Rashmi did not feel guilty about it once she left their lesson and Rebecca's tantrum. Rebecca grew frustrated quickly at learning how to loop the shoelace around the practice nautical cleat, they had spent nearly the whole hour getting Rebecca's confidence back up when she grew frustrated with the instructions. Rashmi had even less confidence in her now, but Guru Geena insisted Rebecca understand the importance of learning the overhead knot so that she could move on to make her own weapon using the mushti knot.

Rashmi moved into a power stance, she would complete this mission and protect Rebecca and The Ladoo Crew. Guru Geena had mentioned she had already spoken to Poppy about trying a different approach and Rebecca was clearly in a much better mood today. Rashmi tapped the workbench lightly with her gada and said, "Chalo, I have something to show you both. No need to clean up, we will be back to finish working on the checklist."

The three women made their way through The LCC to The Ladoo Room and Rashmi escorted Poppy and Rebecca to the first row of seats. The rest of the seats would fill up soon enough. Guru Geena only ever came into The Ladoo Room to observe the students, once word

64

got out that she would be practicing today it would be standing room only. Poppy and Rebecca had saved a seat for Rashmi, thinking she was following them, but Rashmi shook her head from where she stood on the floor, which was always covered with mats to protect the warriors' tumbles as they practiced. Learning to fall and learning to get hit were much more challenging skills to learn than the cleat hitch; this what was Rashmi and Guru Geena wanted Rebecca to understand.

Guru Geena clapped her hands from where she stood, and silence swept across The Ladoo Room. Rashmi saw word had spread and many of the women had interrupted their day and rushed through The LCC to see the special event happening in The Ladoo Room.

"As you all know, The Ladoo Crew has a special client with us," Guru Geena began, "Rebecca, please sit, no one will clap for you."

A few of the women couldn't help but laugh and Rashmi looked over to see Poppy shushing Rebecca, pulling her back into her seat to stop her from storming off. Rashmi wanted to roll her eyes at the thought of Rebecca making it out those doors if The Ladoo Crew wanted to stop her.

"I asked Rashmi if she thought we should give a demonstration of how sweet a ladoo can be for Rebecca and she thought it was a good idea."

Rashmi jogged towards Guru Geena and Guru Geena began to swing her weapon above her head. Two small orange spheres swung in a perfect circle as she held onto a third orange sphere, each orange attached to the other with a length of rope.

"I'll give you a head start," Guru Geena laughed, "Three, two..."

As soon as Rashmi heard Guru Geena say 'three' she began to sprint as fast as she could across the mats to the far side of The Ladoo Room. Before she heard Guru Geena say 'one' she zagged, but it was not done nimbly enough. Rashmi crashed to the mats, Guru Geena's ladoos entangled upon her shins.

"Another?" Guru Geena called to Rashmi.

Rashmi had disentangled herself and stood standing. She whipped Guru Geena's ladoos above her head once before releasing them, Guru Geena catching them perfectly with Rashmi's soft toss.

"No count this time though," Rashmi shouted before charging Guru Geena.

Guru Geena swung the weapon above her head and released it, once again Rashmi came tumbling down, she had fallen face down and her hands were free, but it was not enough. Guru Geena was able to lunge at Rashmi, pulling her back by her hair. She spun Rashmi onto her back and shoved her down to the ground. Guru Geena straddled her good friend's daughter and with one hand holding Rashmi down on the mats, Guru Geena drew her other arm back and her hand formed a fist under custom black brass knuckles, the surface of each shaped like a panther ready to chomp. She stopped just inches in front of Rashmi's throat, ready to interfere with oxygen making its way in and out of her lungs.

Rashmi lay frozen under Guru Geena's mushti mudra. Both women knew if truly pitted against one another, Rashmi would not lay still and wait for death.

"The lessons you think are so stupid or too much work to learn can help you Rebecca," Guru Geena said as she offered Rashmi a hand to stand, "Please consider it."

The rest of The Ladoo Crew dispersed, and Rashmi returned to Poppy and Rebecca. "Let's head back," was all she said.

As the three made their way down the hallway, Rebecca was gushing, "OK, I am not going to lie. That was totally badass, Guru Geena is like, ancient and she almost killed you! Gamps must've been kidding about all that contract stuff, did Gamps send me here to train for a new Slater Corp reality show?"

Rashmi joined Poppy and Rebecca at the workbench and put an end to the exhilaration Rebecca was feeling.

"These knots?" Rashmi shook the laminated instructions at Rebecca, "You can make them over rocks, tennis and lacrosse balls, we could get find some wood, there's the newspaper from your beginners gada, hell, if you train long enough you will get some steel ball bearings when you become part of The Ladoo Crew…But Rebecca, you have to understand that this isn't for some reality show competition. There are people trying to hurt you."

Rebecca rolled her eyes, "They're just fans. That's why I have Slater Corp security wherever I go."

"And if Slater Corp tries to hurt you?" Poppy asked.

Rebecca's face fell, "Gamps."

"And your Gamps hired us."

Rebecca nodded silently, fiddling with the shoelaces in front of her.

"You may be too young to remember this, but your mom, your dad too, Stiles or whatever, they rose to fame at an incredibly unique time in our country's history. We've never had royals, but we wanted them. So, we made our own royalty to worship. It became a lucrative career for many. The magazine publishers, the paparazzi, the stylists, the celebrity's production studios, you know way more than me who all is involved, don't you Rebecca? I am not the expert at how you've been treated by them, you are. Only you know."

Rashmi looked at Rebecca who was furiously referencing the checklist.  Satisfied that Rebecca was sailing through the instructional sheet that had just been shaken at her, Rashmi continued as Rebecca practiced her ties, "As we, the people, wanted to know more and more about our favorite celebrity's life, the cost for that information skyrocketed. Sure, some celebs worked out their own deals with the paparazzi, arranging for them to be where there were going to be, wearing the outfits they had been paid to be seen in, sometimes with another celebrity they *needed* to be seen with. Those celebrities pretended to not want to be photographed.

"Then there were the celebrities who truly did want privacy. They didn't want photos of them wearing no makeup, rolling their trash bins back inside, or fighting with their parents or kids on their birthday. The celebrities who killed or were killed as they drove drunk, trying to outrun the paparazzi. It was all so sad. Especially for the women. They were the ones who were hurt most by our obsession to want to know everything. So, we could pretend we did know them, so that we could be them. And of course, it made it much easier for us to judge them. That's what we loved most about learning about our royalty's lives.

"Around this time, when our obsession with celebrities was beginning to peak, I started work in Geena Auntie's, I mean Guru Geena's, private security firm in college as receptionist. Answering phones, filing paperwork, putting envelopes in the mail, I did anything that Guru Geena asked for help with. All thanks to my mother's friendship with Geena *Auntie*. Back then Geena Auntie wanted her business called *Garbha*, she and the few other women who worked for her would carry two batons, branches, lathi, drumsticks, dandiya, whatever you want to call them. They would use their loud voices and the loud claps of their weapons to force the paparazzi or sometimes the fans to back up from their clients. They would wave them, threatening a beating to anyone who stepped too close to who they were being paid to protect.

"We didn't have too many clients or agents back then, but the pay was really, really good Rebecca. There was no way I could make that much money doing anything else. Especially at my young age. The pay was so good that I deferred my plans for law school to take Geena Auntie's self-defense intensive training. It was offered to me for free, whether it was because I was my mother's daughter or because Guru Geena saw something in me. Whatever the reason, I didn't hesitate when the offer was made.

"Guru Geena couldn't compete with many of the other private security firms. Many of her competitors were former law enforcement, hired directly by celebrities. A lot less overhead compared to Guru Geena's model. She decided to expand her business, offer services that the other private firms either could not or would not.

"While the training was offered to me for free, as the daughter of Geena Auntie's good friend Anjali, others (always rich daughters like you, sent to Geena Auntie by upset millionaire and billionaire fathers) paid Guru Geena a lot of money to stay at this compound, to sleep in these bunk beds, to do their own laundry, to make their own food, to serve one another, to avoid the headache that came with being a celebrity, and learn how to fight. They came here because someone thought they could use Guru Geena's help. With self-discipline.

"*Garbha* wasn't as successful as a security firm to the stars but reestablished as this sort of self-injurious wellness retreat for bad girls, it took off when we rebranded as *The Sweet Retreat*."

Rashmi saw that Rebecca was flying through the first six knots that had been assigned to her days earlier and Poppy had slid over the laminated instructions for knots of an increased difficulty along with the practice nautical hitch. Rashmi continued her plea to Rebecca, "You know exactly how sweet it is here. I attended the trainings and lived as a guest, a client, to learn what they learned. How to protect themselves and how to recognize their own self-worth. I took quickly to the basic skills, just like you are right now, and as I learned what I was capable of, all I could think about was how I wanted to be able to fight back. To attack. It didn't take long before I was invited to attend private training with Guru Geena to learn those skills. I stayed and learned even more from the other women here.

"Guru Geena *wants* us to have those skills, none of us believe they should be kept secret, but we do believe that if you don't have some of these basics down, you could use what you learn to hurt. And several of us came into these trainings *wanting* to hurt, how could we not?

"Guru Geena stresses to us that those who attack are the cause for *The Sweet Retreat*'s existence. No need for self-defense without an attacker, right?

"I wasn't the only one who was more interested in offense than defense though. Once subscribers of those celebrity magazines saw some of the world's most famous people swinging their little mushti knots on their keychains with their iced coffees, those same magazines were advertising our 'wellness center'."

Rashmi looked and only Poppy met her pause, Rebecca was tearing through the rope Poppy had provided to her in order to practice along with the more advanced instructions, "Ana Pearson gave an interview and when asked how her shoulders were so defined, if her arms had gotten so lean from her training for her upcoming adventure film or from her dance practices as she got ready for her residency in Vegas, she told the paparazzi that it was from swinging a ladoo around her head for hours a day. And then it all happened so fast, our success, no one knew us as *Garbha* or *The Sweet Retreat* any longer because *Celebrities We Love,* distributed under Slater Corp publishing, had referred to us as 'trainers with *The Ladoo Crew'.* Just like that our past had been erased by Slater Corp. Soon came *our* peak. Geena Auntie couldn't keep up with the interview requests and without a receptionist, *we* couldn't keep up with the applications from across the country of people who wanted to 'train' with us or who wanted to send their kids here to teach them something that they thought couldn't be taught."

Rashmi paused her story, she wanted to confirm Rebecca was actually listening. Once Rebecca looked up expectantly, she continued, "Whenever interviewed Guru Geena tried to point out the need for *The Ladoo Crew* to exist. That it wasn't all about self-care, or an escape from the day to day, or a reward for busting your ass and not taking care of yourself for weeks or months at a time. That there were women who had a need for these trainings. Because there were people who wanted to hurt them. Because they had never been taught who or what to watch out for. How to be aware of their surroundings. How to know if they were being followed. How to follow someone who was following them. How to manipulate someone into doing what needed to be done. There is so much for you to learn Rebecca. I only imagine what you could do if you train here with us.

"Guru Geena had made connections through all this. She wanted what I am talking to you about right now. She referred to it as 'social orchestrating' when she told me what we could do if we could help the women who come here to understand the power they hold. It sounded too manipulative to me but it also sounded like something Slater Corp had been doing at a scale we could never compete with. Geena Auntie and my own mother Anjali had had to do this with people their whole lives in order to be seen. Only they did it to try and make positive change. I don't like it and I also understand the need for us to try.

"We justify it by saying at least we are showing women their power when they pay us whereas Slater Corp just takes it from them along with their money. We are both selling something, but Guru Geena sells a service I believe in. I don't know if I can convince you Rebecca, but you deserve to know that, especially before you turn 18."

Rashmi threw her palms onto the workbench, shaking the surface Rebecca was practicing on. She wanted to close up, stop wasting their time as she grew frustrated with Rebecca's silence. If Rebecca were this apathetic, what could anyone do to help? Rashmi didn't think she would be able to convince Rebecca that although it was challenging to learn at The LCC, a more difficult challenge was not being able to trust your own instincts. Seeing that Rebecca still held her silence Rashmi sat down beside her, Rebecca was now enveloped on both sides by members of The Ladoo Crew. "Look at us," Rashmi tried to joke, "One, two, three ladoos in a row."

Rashmi grabbed a cord of rope from the work bench and began to fiddle with it, determined to convince Rebecca that she was capable of this, no one had ever told her no, so how was it that Rebecca had been convinced that she shouldn't even try?

Rashmi practiced her ties and spoke once more, "If you still want others to protect you, that's fine Rebecca, it's just that I'd much rather that it was us. The Ladoo Crew is able to charge the fee we do to protect public figures because we do a far better job than some of Guru Geena's competition.

"Guru Geena hand-picked who we would protect and who could stay here. We set up a system so that as more and more women stayed on, wanting to support Guru Geena's vision, we all agreed on selecting which clients needed our help so that *we* could be safe too. We decide together. And even though we can protect ourselves, we are still targets. So having the perspectives of one another helped us help those we had never even met. Guru Geena could tap into the expertise of so experiences in order to select her clients and match them so they could thrive. Meanwhile, competing firms such as our main competitor, Dave Blank, took on as many celebrities as they could and hired anyone who applied to protect them. They wanted to make as much money as possible, which we understand. It's just they didn't care about the cost of doing this work that way. The Ladoo Crew took teaching their clients and protecting them much more seriously. How we handle things matters. Guru Geena makes it clear to all of us that there is little room for mistakes if we want to prosper. At first, we may care most about prospering in our *own* careers and bank accounts, but Ladoo Crew security agents don't get the second chance that a Blank Security agent may get once a mistake is made.

"An agent fired from Blank Security could get a job at almost any other security firm. An agent fired from any security firm could easily get hired at Blake Security. If you're kicked out of The Ladoo Crew, what other security firm to protect women will you go work at? It's near impossible to do it on your own. All of this and more helped Blank Security get paid.

"Jensen Emberly wanted to be seen as a client of The Ladoo Crew, but Guru Geena would not even return his representation's calls because he showed no interest in changing his destructive and often abusive behavior to waitstaff or the general public. Guru Geena believed he just wanted to have an elite security firm photographed with him, and most of us agreed. A few of us thought Jensen could change if he saw what his potential was but Guru Geena and most of us thought he had had plenty of opportunities to know his value and his potential.

Jensen's representation thought it would be good for him to be immersed with us, that we would influence him, but Guru Geena had to consider what was good for The Ladoo Crew first. She told his representatives to contact her in a few months, once Jensen began to care a bit more about how he presented himself to the world, or when he acted like the person he *said* he wanted to be. But Jensen wasn't interested in changed behavior, he just wanted more attention. Any way he could get it. So, he went with whoever would take him and Blank Security jumped at the opportunity. I told you it was good pay.

"Blank Security staff escorted Jensen on his European tour and while there, stood aside to 'protect' their client from the staff of the war memorial where young women had once been hidden by their families, escaping threats of work camps for nearly two years, their families' attempt to keep them safe from the work camps that became extermination camps, set up by the fascists ruling their country and the collaborators that let it occur.

"Blank Security physically held back the staff of the memorial so that Jensen could write his name with permanent black marker on the walls of the small closet the young girls had tried to survive in. Jensen Emberly's career wasn't over because of that incident, you of all people must know he co-hosts that dumb bad boy reality show on Slater TV. How old is Jensen now Poppy?" Rashmi asked.

"Hmm, he must be 32, 33?" Poppy replied as she worked alongside Rebecca and Rashmi, practicing her ties.

"Ahh yes, an adult man hosting a show titled *Boys will be Boys.* But would he be host today if Guru Geena had accepted him? Maybe this was what he wanted for his future; it is an easy job after all. Such a pathetic display of disrespect all for some attention and to be a blip on a news cycle for a minute or two. That news coverage would have never happened if Guru Geena had accepted Jensen Emberly as a client. But she never would have. She refused to even meet with his management because his reputation preceded him.

"You know who else we couldn't help Rebecca? Bethany Kohl, you've heard of her, I'm sure," Rashmi had been watching Rebecca and noticed that she had leaned in a little bit, maybe a sign that she now held her attention, that maybe Rebecca was listening intently as she continued to learn how to tie her knots.

"Guru Geena *had* accepted high risk Bethany as a client, even though her conduct could be seen as similar to Jensen. Bethany could easily afford a driver but continued to drive drunk, the paparazzi photographing her multiple car crashes, the celebrity magazines loving her mug shots. She dressed up for them, you know.

"Her father, Abe Kohl, was redeeming an IOU Geena Auntie had given him when he used his power as Secretary of Health Services to help all of The Ladoo Crew get regular access to the Hog Flu vaccine at no cost so we would not be at risk when protecting clients. Guru Geena would have wanted Bethany to show she wanted to change her life before first accepting her as a client, but she didn't have much say if she wanted to keep us safe during those first pandemics.

"I had been the one personally assigned as lead to Bethany Kohl's security detail, selected by Secretary Kohl himself. Guru Geena knew she could trust me, that if Secretary Kohl tried to hire me personally, I would use it to The Ladoo Crew's advantage. I wanted more than money. I still do. I try to get others to see that. I didn't even get to try with Bethany, but I tried to try. I really did," Rashmi set the thick rope she had tied into a chain sinnet down and placed her palms on top of it, flattening it against the workbench. Rashmi pulled the links tight in place, clearing her throat before beginning to speak once more, "I advised Bethany against dating certain men in the influence circles she chose to socialize in. But I was continually dismissed; Bethany thought her father had hired me to be her friend, to do what *she* wanted and what she still wanted was to be seen. She could have been anything or done anything she wanted. But the thing is, and I think you already know this about me Rebecca, if I had been hired to be her friend, I still would have said the same thing. Isn't that what you want from your friends? To tell you when you're being a clown?

"When I knew for certain that Bethany did not want to hear what I was advising, I reported so much to Guru Geena. Guru Geena then addressed Bethany's refusal to respect courting recommendations directly with Secretary Kohl. To be blunt, we were never concerned with the number of Bethany's hook ups, we were concerned about the men Bethany consistently chose to hook up with. Bethany wanted excitement and drama. Like Jensen, she wanted attention and to be a blip on a news cycle. Secretary Kohl didn't care what she did, but he wished The Ladoo Crew could just make his daughter stop being such a bother. To Guru Geena's face Bethany's father acted as though he had a high opinion of any of The Ladoo Crew's recommendations but when he spoke with his daughter, never addressing the difficulties she was facing *and* creating, it was made clear to The Ladoo Crew that he thought of us more as babysitters than experts in force and tactics. Women fighting to create a new world for all. Secretary Kohl valued making his daughter happy in the near future more than his daughter's or all children's happiness in the long run. Secretary Kohl preferred to take it easy, he did not like telling his daughter 'no' or that she was making a mistake. He didn't want to deal with her and knowing he was ignoring our pleas to remove her from the lifestyle she was chasing, even just for a bit really limited what we could do to help her. What could we do to make them hear us?

"Once Bethany began dating extremist political 'influencer' Tanner Heart, I worried about having to tell Guru Geena that I didn't think we should continue on as Bethany's security detail. That we should quit. I thought she would be disappointed with my leadership, disappointed that I wanted to give up. But my worry was for nothing. I should have known that Guru Geena recognized that sometimes you have to leave. Lose. Guru Geena trusted what I had told her. That Secretary Kohl had given up. He had chosen to be polite to his daughter when we had asked him to show her love.

"Knowing that we would be leaving Bethany with a father who simply considered her another obligation hurt us all, but we didn't know what else we could do. Guru Geena contacted Secretary Kohl to inform him that she was immediately pulling The Ladoo Crew from Bethany's security detail, claiming that his daughter had violated an initialed clause The Ladoo Crew required of everyone under their protection. The Ladoo Crew refused to protect anyone who actively incited violence in any way, including through hate speech.

"Tanner was well known for using hate to grab a claim to fame. There were dating pre-screen or background checks needed on Tanner, something that was commonly done by all the security firms that public figures hire. They wanted to know who they were letting into their lives. The Ladoo Crew didn't have to dig down deep, Tanner had no shame. He was proud of all he had ever done.

"Jensen Emberly's idiotic act at the war memorial wouldn't have been enough to cause Guru Geena to pause Bethany's contract. At the time. We saw it as an act of ignorance, as he was cheered on by the wrong people, having been a child star who continued to skyrocket towards fame. I must be naïve to believe that Emberly could have done more good in his life than host *Boys will be Boys*, with all the money, power, and fame he had been given, with the head start he had been given, if only he had had a few people who told him 'no' in his life. *I love you so much I am telling you no.*

"I thought of Jensen as simply a child who had grown with no guidance. Tanner," Rashmi nearly growled his name, "did what he did because of hate. He had been convinced that he didn't have what he deserved because it had been taken from him and then successfully used all of his social media accounts to gain 'influence' by posing in different locales while making a salute associated with genocide and femicide. Tanner rode a tidal wave to power by preaching that those of us that are the weak were taking from those like him, the strong.

"Tanner's philosophies were popular with those who felt they were being plotted against, denied what was owed to them, gaining followers quickly on multiple social media platforms. He became a legitimate journalist somehow, saying he spoke the truth, straight to his followers, eventually becoming editor of P2BE magazine, a magazine no one heard of until Tanner Heart became editor," Rashmi chuckled to herself, nothing mirthful, more at the absurdity of it all. Rebecca and Poppy both looked at Rashmi, so she drew herself together and continued, knowing this may be her last chance with Rebecca, that she had to get to the point, "Proud To Be Elite, it's rarely referred to by its official title anymore. A yearly newsletter for those who were descendants of The Elite. The superior to the inferior. That fucking newsletter had almost died and was resurrected to become the monster machine that it is today, possibly because The Ladoo Crew quit. Because I quit. I will always wonder if things would be different if I could have figured out a way to torment Tanner out of Bethany's life. I'll never understand why it has to upset the balance the way it does, for The Ladoo Crew to do what we do. They really can't stand to hear us say, 'I love *myself* so much I am telling you no.'"

Rashmi paused, gathering herself after contemplating her past. She may never come to terms with it. She couldn't say she would choose a different path today, as sad as the story was. There was nothing she could have done to get Bethany to see who Tanner really was. To show Bethany what Tanner was really after. Rashmi would always feel guilty for leaving Bethany with Tanner and she was over replaying the past as though she was the only one who could have stopped what happened.

Rashmi refused to be the only one who held that burden, she pulled her chain sinnet apart with her fingers, explaining to Rebecca and Poppy, "There was nothing The Ladoo Crew could have done to break those two up. Bethany had her reasons and Tanner had his. Secretary Kohl had come to us several times for help after we dropped them as clients, even while he was still working with Blank Security; and still after Blank Security was bought out by Slater Corporation. Former

Secretary Kohl came to us after he realized Blank Security wasn't as interested in protecting his daughter as they were in protecting Tanner.

"Blank Security staff loved everything Tanner had to say and if they didn't, they still took the paycheck. I watched as Guru Geena made a mistake - because we fuck up too Rebecca, I watched her lecture Secretary Kohl, telling him that his daughter had made a decision and now, seeing that she was an adult after all, she would have to live with it. That the mess was too big for The Ladoo Crew to clean up. I didn't have the confidence to disagree with Guru Geena. She was my mother's good friend, and I was raised to respect my elders. Geena Auntie may have made mistakes, but Guru Geena never did. That is what I told myself, to stay quiet, that Guru Geena doesn't make mistakes," Rashmi laughed again, "I had wanted to suggest that Secretary Kohl pull Bethany out from Blank Security's protection, just like we've done for you and Slater Corp, and send her to one of our upcoming self-defense camps. To force Bethany to stay at The LCC for as many months as it took to deprogram her from Tanner's sick *philosophies*. Once Bethany was out of her estate, it would take nothing for Secretary Kohl to kick out Tanner and Blank Security.

"There was a lot we could have done, yes, The Ladoo Crew, we have beaten ourselves up with shame about how we could have made other choices and also, I know you know what happened next. The arrow was already in motion, headed towards its target. Tanner is a host on Slater News Channel, your dad has been on his show, shaking his hands at those elite dinners they get invited to. Tanner is just here now, one of the people who inform *us*. Secretary Kohl? No one thinks about him anymore, his political career over, Tanner ruined it when he ruined Bethany's life. She went back to him, again and again, putting up with the abuse. Once he was able to grab the next rung on the ladder, he left, and she did too.

"I wish she could have known that if she felt alone, she could have been alone with us. The arrow was in motion and The Ladoo Crew was not there for her. We thought there was one rule that had to apply to everyone who needed our help. Later we talked about it, I finally trusted myself enough to speak to Geena Auntie, telling her that we couldn't abandon people who need our help like this, and Geena Auntie didn't even have to steady herself. She looked me right in the eyes to tell me that if it all happened again, she would do everything the same because she was certain that Blank Security had been working *with* Secretary Kohl and Tanner. Blank Security is owned by Slater Corp, it was all too much, and we weren't ready. Guru Geena stood by her decision. They all worked together, even after all Tanner had done to his daughter, Secretary Kohl went on his show because he hadn't wanted his own career to end. His daughter had been an obligation that got in the way of his aspirations instead of helping him achieve them.

"The Ladoo Crew could have kidnapped Bethany and helped protect her from the abusive environment that she was in with Tanner, but Secretary Kohl would not have done a thing to stop Tanner and his P2BE minions from spreading their hate. There were so many photos of Secretary Kohl with Tanner *before* he got his show. His presence in Secretary Kohl's life made him look like a legitimate political advisor when the only life, political, educational, or career experience he could ever claim was self-knowledge. As though he had created bigotry, misogyny, and xenophobia; came up with it all on his own," Rashmi scoffed.

"I have a question," Rebecca interjected.

Poppy and Rashmi both nodded. Rashmi's eyes grew wide as she anticipated Rebecca's query about the history of The Ladoo Crew.

Rebecca had perfected her overhand knot; she had left about eight inches as a tail. Both Poppy and Rashmi later confirmed that Rebecca's eyes had indeed flashed before she began swinging the ladoo over her head by its tether, asking her instructors, "Have you like, ever set one of these on fire before you tossed it?"

# Chapter Twelve

Kavita finished washing the remaining dirty dishes while Gayatri transferred that evening's dinner into containers that made it easier for Neil to carry to the leeches. Rice in sealed plastic containers, the dal and tomato curry into their own crockpots. The paratha was already wrapped up; Kavita always made those in big batches and wrapped them in wax paper and tin foil, ten per wrap, stacked in columns on the bottommost shelf of the fridge. The leeches could warm those up on their own if they wanted. Kavita served her free food two ways: take it or leave it.

As Kavita washed the oily pots at the double sinks, she noticed one of the leeches stand up from his seat at one of the picnic tables. He began to approach the patio doors. Kavita began to sweat. She had told Neil time and time again that if he was going to allow these losers to hang out doing nothing all day, they had to stay away from the house. She wanted nothing to do with them and knew they all wanted something from her. In that moment she hated her older brother for wanting so desperately to fit in. Kavita laughed to herself as she thought about how she always told Anand he could do whatever he wanted, he was learning the most valuable skill, how to march to his own beat. She was stressed, she knew her little brother should have made it to the compound by now, so it was only a matter of time before Neil found out she wanted to leave. That she didn't feel safe. And that she was going to try and take Gayatri. There was no way she was going to leave her niece with a man who looked to guidance from men like Nick and boys like the leeches when it came to how to treat women and how to raise young girls.

Kavita scared herself as she heard Gayatri's chair squeak from movement, causing her to drop the towel she used to dry off her hands into the still wet sink. Kavita took a moment to steady herself and then made her way to stand in between the glass patio doors and Gayatri who continued to help pack up food for the leeches.

Kavita watched as the leech approached, he smiled wistfully at his crush and waved at her through the door. It was Alfie, one of Neil's younger friends, the one Neil was always trying to encourage Kavita to 'get to know'.

"You deserve to have a good time Kavita, have some kids of your own. He wants to ask you out, you'll at least get a free meal," Neil had said two nights ago at dinner.

"I'm busy that night," was her response.

Alfie stood smiling sheepishly through the glass door, he reminded Kavita of a dog who had accidentally got locked out of the house.

"Dinner isn't ready yet," Kavita said through the closed door, "Neil will get it out to you once he gets home." She moved to close the vertical blinds in order to end the conversation. She didn't want Alfie to have a chance to speak.

"Hold up!" Alfie shouted through the door, "I got something I wanted to ask you."

'Here it comes,' Kavita thought, planning a misdirect to get her niece out of the kitchen. She did not want Gayatri to witness Alfie's anger when she told him no. She held up her hand to Alfie's face while she asked Gayatri to run to the dining room to grab a few thalis, stored in the mahogany credenza her parents had bought after they first purchased this home. "See if there's anything else we could use to help us make decorations for the party, we'll use the big pad of paper," she raised her voice to tell Gayatri as she ran off. Kavita knew the credenza was a mess and Gayatri would waste plenty of time exploring it, seeing what was in there that they could trace or use to decorate for her party.

"What do you want?" Kavita asked, wondering if she should chop some cucumbers just so she'd have a knife in her hand if she needed it.

"You know how Gaya has her birthday at the bowling alley this weekend?" Alfie began before Kavita interrupted him.

"What birthday party? At Nick's bowling alley?" Kavita asked incredulously. Neil hadn't said a word to her and just last night she told him how she planned on making pizza from scratch with the girls so Gayatri could have a pizza party with her sisters. Neil didn't let her go to school, who would he have invited to her party? And it was the same weekend as his damn Salute to Straights Parade.

"Oh, I thought you knew," Alfie fumbled over his words.

"Are you sure there's a party tomorrow?" Kavita asked. She was baffled by Alfie's approach. She knew this was something that Neil would do to her, make a decision like this to force her to go out with his friend but still could not believe he actually had done so.

"Yes, there definitely is Kav-eeta," Alfie affirmed as he mispronounced her name. Kavita bristled at this, moving back slightly from the glass door. She knew he had been sitting with his friends, practicing how to ask her out; Neil had talked him into it, she was sure. But Alfie couldn't take the time to listen to how Neil pronounced her name. Neil never corrected Alfie when he spoke about her.

Alfie met Kavita's silence and spoke a little louder, "Well I figured you'd be there, and I'd be there so uh, you'd want to go together."

Kavita wanted to close her eyes as she wondered why he would figure that? But she knew it was because Neil was pushing her on him. Kavita really did not like that Alfie wasn't asking, he was telling.

Kavita exhaled a heavy sigh. "Well, I didn't know about the party so must not have been invited. Neil definitely would have told me if he wanted me there. And I wouldn't want to make anyone mad, it's rude to go when you aren't invited, you know?" Kavita said, rushing to end this conversation.

"Oh! Um, we can fix that, let's think," Alfie was taken aback, he and his friends had probably not planned for Kavita not knowing about the party.

Kavita knew that Neil wouldn't have expected her to decline an event where she'd get to see all of her nieces. "Oh, that's alright Alfie.

Have a good night," she said before she began to draw the vertical blinds shut.

"Wait Kav-eeta! I'm inviting you then! You'll be my date!" Alfie beamed at her.

Kavita stopped closing the blinds and stood at the glass door, watching Alfie smile as though he didn't have a worry in the world. Kavita had reached the end of her patience. "You don't think it's rude you're inviting me to my own family's party?" Kavita scowled at him.

Alfie frowned and began to complain, "Listen don't take that out on me. Neil is the head of your family and I'm respecting his wishes. I don't butt into another man's business. I'm just asking you out, it's not like you have a lot of options, Kav-eeta." Alfie shook his head in disbelief at how he was being treated.

Kavita opened her mouth to respond as Gayatri came running into the kitchen, her hands stacked full of metal thalis, cups, and tiffins. She skidded to a stop and the metal all came crashing to the kitchen floor. Gayatri shouted, "I need help!" over the cacophony of the metal reverberating on the tiles.

Kavita took the corded loop that opened and closed the vertical blinds for the glass patio in her hands and shrugged at Alfie. She smiled apologetically at him as she closed the blinds on him. Kavita knew there'd be repercussions for what just happened, but she kept the smile on her face as they stood there, knowing he could fully see that smile was not in her eyes.

Once the blinds were completely closed Kavita still stood there frozen, wondering how long she would have to stand there silently. She wanted so badly to peek through the blinds to make sure Alfie wasn't still standing there waiting for her. She felt she had to plan for whatever his next move may be. Would he knock on the glass and ask her out again? Would he wait on the porch for Neil to come home to tell on her before she could tell on *him*?

Gayatri crawled towards Kavita and reached up to pull on her shirt. "It's my birthday weekend, what's he going to do? Put dad in a bad mood?" Gayatri whispered.

Kavita exhaled all the breath she had been holding as she realized Gayatri was probably right. Kavita felt an urgency to rush to the kitchen sink to close the horizontal blinds so the leeches couldn't look in but kept her cool, walking calmly to the sink and observing the leeches circling Alfie as he told them his tale of what just happened. As Kavita closed those shades she thought about how she didn't know Alfie at all. They'd never even spoken other than the most basic of greetings. Right now Alfie could be bragging to his friends she said yes, or he could be telling them she said she wasn't invited. Kavita could not recall if she had actually told him no. Would he understand that she did not want to go out with him? That she wished he would leave her alone?

Kavita motioned to Gayatri to join her, "Ok, time to clean up this mess now." Kavita and Gayatri began to crawl on the floor, picking up the dishes that had spilt to the floor in rescue. "We have time for one more tale before your dad comes home and we eat," Kavita began, pointing to the tapestry, "Durga's bow represents all the potential energy she controls, and the arrow represents all of the kinetic energy she has under her control. Durga controls all aspects of energy. Potential is what's stored and kinetic is what's in motion, ok?

"After that sillie billie Saaya left Frank's foxhole, they began to spy on the humans. Saaya wanted to learn more about the humans in order to help their friends in the forest. Saaya decided to investigate the road the humans would travel upon. For a long time Saaya simply observed, marveling at the hustle and bustle the humans put effort into each day. Over time Saaya noticed an older woman who traveled the path to the market each day from the town. Each morning the woman would walk one direction with an empty basket and return each afternoon with a partially full one.

"One day Saaya stopped their watch as they noticed a new sound on the road. As Saaya strained to recognize the sound they noticed the woman. She was pushing a cart with one wheel, balancing so many belongings on it that she could barely see over the top of it. Saaya watched as she traveled slowly, stopping to walk back and pick up a thing or two which had fallen from the objects she had stacked as carefully as possible. Equilibrium only occurring when the cart was stopped, never when it was in motion.

"Saaya moved from his perch in order to inventory the woman's belongings. With their green eyes squinted, Saaya noted exquisitely embroidered blankets and shawls, metal thalis, and tiffins, just like we have here. Oh, and carved sandalwood boxes which clinked as the cart moved, making Saaya think that there were even more of the woman's trinkets inside. Saaya waited for the woman's return from the market and that afternoon she walked back with nothing, not even the cart that had carried her belongings!

"Saaya waited the next day for the woman and was confused when the woman did not travel her route. Saaya washed their paws and told themselves they simply continue to watch the road, observing so they could learn more. As time went on, Saaya noted that the woman no longer walked the route. Saaya did nothing for he only set out to observe and learn and he had just learned something: sometimes that just happened with the humans.

"After a few weeks, Saaya began a new routine in order to learn even more about the humans hunting in the forest. Saaya continued to keep watch, examining different parts of the forest at different points in the day. One day Saaya paused on their route in order to observe the woman who had returned with no cart, she was replacing a pile of rocks. Because Saaya was their name, the woman did not notice Saaya spying.

"Now that Saaya had picked up on this woman's new routine, they changed their own. Saaya continued to watch the main road during peak travel times to learn about all the humans, and also made an effort each day to check the woman's pile of rocks, to learn about this individual human. Every day Saaya would observe the woman peer at

85

her pile of rocks, watching her separate the carefully piled rocks from one another and then putting them back together, in almost the same exact order as she had begun with, before leaving them once again. Always looking back longingly towards her pile of stones. Each day the woman did this, through almost two whole seasons in the forest. Every day Saaya would check over the pile of rocks as they made their rounds, guarding the forest, but Saaya never inspected the stones themselves; Saaya was convinced it must be some sort of a trap.

"One day, Saaya arrived earlier than usual to secretly supervise the rock removal and reinstatement when *another* human showed up. This was a younger woman in a different colored cloak. She removed the stones and then took some of the items from the pile, shoving them into the pockets of her cloak. Once the rock pile had been strewn about sufficiently, this other woman ran away, clutching her cloak to her body. Saaya never once saw her look back longingly at the stones. Saaya had an urge to chase this new woman, to learn about her but decided to stay put. Saaya had yet to witness good come to an animal of the forest who interfered with the affairs of humans.

"Saaya jumped up to one of their highest spots, one where they could spy without being seen and sure enough the who once had a cart came through the forest, running towards her spot once she saw the rocks thrown across the earth. The woman saw her pile of rocks was no more and lost her balance, falling to her knees as she sobbed.

"Saaya's curiosity tugged so hard at them that they broke their vow to only observe. Saaya mewed from their spot in their tree in order to get the woman's attention. Once the woman looked up Saaya asked her if she was having trouble piling the stones back on top of one another.

"The woman kneeled on the earth, her shoulders sagged, and she clutched a rock in each hand. Saaya watched as the woman lifted her chin and began to howl so loudly that all of the starlings left their roosts and flew away, shifting in formations as one cloud to escape their predators.

"'You. Dumb. Cat!' the woman screamed, throwing a rock at the tree, missing Saaya by a long shot, the rock landing far from the tree's vicinity.

"'Don't throw stones at me!' Saaya hissed, 'I was only wondering about the game you play with your friend.'

"'My friend?!' the woman asked in disbelief.

Saaya nodded before licking their paws in order to clean their mane.

"'Whoever touched these rocks is no friend of mine!' the woman cried out, challenging Saaya's claim, now pushing out her chest at them as she huffily told the cat, 'I sold everything I had in exchange for gold bangles. I could wear them if I needed to move from the village quickly or I could sell them one or two at a time so I would always have some money if I needed it!'

"'My pal Frank heard humans keep their gold in their homes and in armed fortresses called banks so that they have it secured at all times. For when they need to spend it, Frank taught me. I don't have a need for gold or banks or homes so I'm not sure what 'spending it' really means but that Frank is a very smart fellow -,' Saaya tried to explain to the distraught woman, but could not as she had begun throwing stones at the feline once again.

"'Why would I spend it?!' the woman screamed as she lunged at Saaya, 'I wanted to always have it!'

"'If you didn't need to spend it, then why did you need it at all? You never planned to spend it, you only wanted to fantasize your riches' potential. Come! I'll help you; I can supervise as you put your pile of rocks together and then you can look inside and imagine your gold bangles are there and everything you sold for them too. You'll see it still feels the same!'"

Kavita and Gayatri stood next to one another at the counter, the metal dishes all stacked, ready to be washed. Kavita pointed at Gayatri, telling her, "Potential can be wasted if you don't plan to use it or tend to it properly."

Gayatri looked up at Kavita, she had been wanting to tell her something. She had been losing sleep worried about what Kavita would think of her if she asked but Gayatri thought that this story must be a sign. Gayatri opened her mouth, she didn't want to lose this moment to tell Kavita that what she wanted for her tenth birthday was for Kavita to adopt her. So that they could move away from Neil and the men he called his friends. Gayatri decided that she would tell her Aunt Kavita her birthday wish and just as she opened her mouth to do so, the phone on the kitchen wall rang.

# Part Three

# Chapter Thirteen

Anand could see one of the compound's fence posts from here. There was a sign, 'No Trespassing'. It was far away but he didn't need to be that close to read the message. The graphic on the sign coupled with the (at least) twelve-foot-high steel palisade fencing (topped with trident speared tips) could not be misunderstood.

Anand felt relief that he could now finally rest being so close to his final destination. Soon he'd be dry and well fed. He hoped. He had to keep hope that The Ladoo Crew would help him help Kavita and Gayatri because if they rejected him when he showed up at their gate, he had no one else to go to for help. He'd be forced to leave Shepherd County and figure out life on his own or return to join Neil and Nick's gang of leeches. Anand had to keep up hope.

He readied to take a break on a damp looking log. He thought about using one of the towels Kavita had packed so he'd have somewhere dry to sit, remembering he'd have warm, dry towels soon enough. If things worked out how he hoped. If the women warriors let him in. The rumor the leeches told about them was that they allowed no unescorted men in their compound, within their fenced walls. Anand started to take the last sip from his water bottle and decided against it. He had to be smart. He couldn't just hope.

Anand placed his bottle on the forest floor, without the cap on. He sat down on the wet log and listened to the call of nature. He heard the song of the wind, a whistle of its own and a harmony with the trees. Anand explored the song of the wind further, finding a melody, transforming the song once he felt one with the song of the water running through Canary Creek. Anand tuned himself into the song of the forest. He felt the chorus run through him and then felt goosebumps pepper his skin as he heard the sound of a few drops land on the log next to him.

*Drip. Drip. Drop.*

*Drip. Drip. Drop.*

He heard a different tone, metallic as the water landed on a large stone.

*Tink. Tink. Tink.*

A drop landed on the crown of Anand's head, he felt it reverberate through his jaw as he heard the individual noise it made, echoing throughout his body.

*Thudt.*

Anand looked at his nearly empty water bottle, willing it to fill before remembering he could.

He took his wizard's staff and looked to the sky, playing a new song, working his magic, orchestrating the heavens. Anand began to clap his wizard's staff, alternating first against the earth and then against the damp log, not sure if his magic would work when he was so desperate. Anand begged for hope as he begged for a rain shower.

# Chapter Fourteen

Poppy had slipped Rashmi a thumbs up as she told her and Rebecca goodbye and that she'd see them at dinner. Rashmi had been just as pleased as Poppy, she had assumed that Rebecca would rather be with her parents and with Slater Corp. Rashmi knew all about fight, flight, or freeze. She had assumed that Rebecca would feel stuck and want to stay with what she had known her whole life. Rashmi had been taught by Guru Geena that if we feel paralyzed, we may choose to do nothing. Rebecca wanting to stay with the people she was familiar with had been one possibility. Rashmi was personally incredibly happy Rebecca had chosen to fight but she was happiest Rebecca hadn't chosen fawn. No approach was perfect, there was simply reaction and every woman The Ladoo Crew protected made the best choice for themselves when offered one. Rashmi just always rooted really hard that their guests would select fight because that's what she would choose. To fight for the world, they wanted.

Rashmi was so delighted with her success she was fighting the urge to whoop loudly down the hall, high fiving other women on their way to the briefing room. She was certain that Guru Geena would know her effort in The Ladoo Room had been worth it as soon as she saw Rashmi walk in. Rashmi wanted badly to pick Geena Auntie up and swing her around and laughed out loud as she remembered Rebecca's instinct to set the ladoos on fire. To learn more about Rebecca through her asking that question was both hilarious and exhilarating. Rashmi could not wait to update her crew, but she'd have to pull it together first. It was only with composure that she could rally The Ladoo Crew with a speech on how there was nothing abnormal about holding anger towards your energy. That they could teach Rebecca to *not* choose violence. That there were practices they all learn so that anger is not acted upon without careful reflection.

Rashmi was able to steer her mood and calm her excitement but still could not help but stroll into the briefing room with a knowing grin for Guru Geena. Her face fell when she saw Guru Geena paid no attention to the entrance as she normally did, watching to see which Ladoo Crew member was the last to file in so that she could instruct them to shut the door. If you were late, she always made a big deal, asking why you thought your time was more valuable than hers. Guru Geena was always ready to lecture the women on wasting time, obsessed with death she hated wasting her most valuable resource.

Johanna, Norah, and Guru Geena were at the conference table and the television was on, a rare occurrence before dinner. Guru Geena preferred to watch the compilation of news updates after everyone was back in the dorm, so her mood wouldn't be soured as she made her rounds, eating a few bites with as many tables as possible so that she could initiate a relationship with every potential recruit. She wanted to come across as easygoing, a cheerleader for the women in her care. Some nights she visited more tables than others, depending on how interesting the conversation was with each group.

The recording being played was muted; the women watched the chryons scroll past as the last few Ladoo Crew members filed into the room. Rashmi sank into her seat and grasped the arms of her chair as she began to read.

*Assassination attempt on state Governor Melinda Fanning while shopping at her local grocery store. 17 critically injured. 4 pronounced dead. Ex-girlfriend of local gunman reported to local authorities her concerns about what the gunman was planning.*

Johanna leaned her head in, pointing to the newscast and whispered, "Our reports say police investigated the ex, claiming she was having a mental health crisis and needed to be evaluated, while apologizing to the gunman when he told them he didn't appreciate the police showing up unannounced."

Rashmi shook her head in disapproval and locked her grip on the arms of her chair, stiffening, she was sweating, her body temperature rising as quickly as her good mood vacated her mind. Just moments earlier she had been certain she would be lifting The Ladoo

Crew's spirits with her update on Rebecca but as she looked around the room and saw the downcast expressions on everyone's faces, she knew she needed to pull back. There was nothing to celebrate.

As the updates rolled along the bottom of the screen, Rashmi watched Tanner Heart speak excitedly, he may as well have been frothing at the mouth. His eyes were gleaming and the women who were watching all noted his attempt at reigning in his hummingbird like energy as he made a steeple with his index fingers, his attempt to look poised. Professional. The muted recording updated to a split screen, Tanner on one side and Leonard Steel on the other. Seeing everyone who needed to be there was present, Guru Geena paused the recording to get everyone's attention before speaking, "I hate his voice as much as you all do but unfortunately, we must hear what he has to say so that we can be prepared to help ourselves and our clients."

With the volume on, and Guru Geena pressed play and the women began to listen, unable to contain their reactions as they looked at one another making faces as the two men spoke. Steel would be coming to Shepherd County to speak to the victims and their families and recruit good guys with guns to join the AmBackPats tonight, or at the Salute to Straights Parade he would now be speaking at this weekend.

"You know what happened tonight was an absolute tragesty," Steel said to Tanner, who did not even notice that Steel had combined two words to make a new one, likely unintentionally, "I hate to say it, but someone has to. This man was a bad guy with a gun, and we needed a good guy with a gun to help stop him. His girlfriend, who had been living with him, tried to protect herself but he intimidated the law enforcement officers who showed up to help them. Women need our help Tanner. I am sorry for everything that happened to Governess Fanning tonight but unfortunately, with women in charge, this is the type of oversight that occurs. The police did all that they could to help the gunman's girlfriend. With women in charge, this means we as a state are doing things that have never been done, traditionally. We need to come to grips with reality, there is a reason why it's called *women's work,"* Steel's jaw set as he said those two words. He paused before continuing, "With Governess Fanning in charge of this state, this means women shopping at night and unfortunately the need to protect women, like the Governess herself, from the bad guys who want to hurt them. I mean really Tanner, do you think something like this could ever happen to me?"

Tanner leaned in, shaking his head at the idea. Tanner wished so badly that Steel was sharing this as a private conversation with him, not acting on camera, and asked, "And what is your plan to protect women? I mean, you'd think for all the crying these feminists do, they would have figured this out by now. They've had several decades to prove themselves but isn't this proof that what they want isn't working? It's just not natural because there will always be bad guys, right? They need *our* help stopping them." Tanner cocked his head, indicating his disdain for the women he disagreed with.

"Thank you, Tanner, that's exactly it," Steel said as Tanner silently nodded his head, agreeing with himself. Steel settled in his chair as he looked directly at the viewers at home, "My plan to keep the women of this great State safe, when elected Governor, would be to enforce an eight pm curfew for women. There's really no reason for them to be out unless they are working. And we need to really think about what kind of job would require a woman to work past eight pm *outside of her home*? Evenings are meant to be spent together as a family. If women want to work after eight pm, they still can if their employer requests it. The employer would pay for a woman's evening work permit; helping to generate revenue for the state. This is really a win-win. There are a lot of underemployed men in this state who could safely work evenings. We are putting the power back into the hands of the employers of this state to improve our citizens lives. We can only do this together."

Tanner's eyes had shone brightly as he took in Steel's proposal and offered Steel a leading statement, steering his candidate's 'interview', "Tell our viewers at home more about what *we* can do to prevent the violence that we saw tonight at the Shepherd County supermarket."

"Yes Tanner," Steel spoke confidently, "In addition to the curfew, I am encouraging all citizens, men *and* women to work together to learn how to protect themselves. I am headed to Shepherd County tonight, unfortunately because of the tragesty at this supermarket. But there is some good that will come of this. I will finally be able to meet a great patriot of this state in person." The video recording now showed footage of Nick, dressed in his militia costume, emblazoned with a patch reading 'Nick's', handing out plastic bottles of water, with multiple weapons visible as he did so.

"Your viewers at home are seeing Nicholas Huber, a patriot my team has been speaking with and who has been organizing in his own community. Nick is a leader here with Americans Back Patriots, right here in Shepherd County, and has been setting an example for all, as far as I'm concerned. He worked with his friends and employees to organize a response to the shooting. Supporting law enforcement, first responders, and with the help of his compatriots, is making sure no one who is not supposed to be here, is here.

"Nick here has been working hard with the community to organize Shepherd County's very first Salute to Straights Parade. I invite all to join us, to march alongside with us *against* this hate that led to tonight's violence."

"And how would marching with AmBackPats help? That seems like something that rarely accomplishes anything," Tanner prodded.

"We, the people, gathering is what accomplishes *everything*," Steel replied, thrusting his words at the viewers, "Everything great requires a sacrifice, and we need to sacrifice what we can afford to. You may sacrifice your weekend to march as with Salute to Straights to keep the women of this state safe. You may be like Nick and sacrifice your time and money to support those who need it, like he's doing right now.

I wish that everyone could be like me and run for office to make the change they want to see, and I hope to see more of that."

Rashmi scoffed. If it weren't disruptive to the others, she would have bitterly laughed out loud. She knew others must feel the same and that at least Norah would have applauded sarcastically at the idea that Steel wanted competition at the ballot box. That he trusted voters to select the proper people to be in charge. Rashmi stayed silent, always careful of what Guru Geena may think of the example she was setting, imagining rolling her eyes like Rebecca, at no one, as she thought about how if it were legal, Steel would assign his associates as mayors, sheriffs, school board appointees, for any and all elected positions so that he could implement his agenda with no opposition.

Rashmi returned her attention to Steel's interview, annoyed that she had to hear Tanner speak again, "I couldn't agree with you more CEO Steel. We all need to do what we can to make this state better. Now, if our viewers attend the Salute to Straights parade, will there be time set aside for you at the rally? An opportunity for citizens to voice their concerns to you as their potential new governor?"

Steel replied with a booming laugh, "I am looking forward to hearing the concerns of our people this weekend, the only thing I am looking forward to more is actually *doing something* about those concerns. The rally is for the people, not for me. And to that end, I *know* that my enemies will spin this to make it look like I am taking advantage of tonight's tragesty, but I had been thinking this was necessary for a very long time now. I'm sad that we need it but glad that we are able to do so. My focus is currently helping the people of this state and when I went to Slater Corporation to tell them, the entire organization was ready to help me, help *us*. Slater Corporation is excited to announce that we will be adding a new channel for all Slater TV subscribers - starting next week, get ready for *Strong as Steel TV*.

"I've felt that the people of this country, this state, this county, you viewers watching right now, *your* ideas are the ones that will solve our problems. On *Strong as Steel TV* you'll be able to talk directly to me, nightly, letting me know what needs to be done to improve your lives. Has Governess Fanning ever come to you? Will she be able to now?

"I am a busy man, but not so busy I don't have the time to listen to the needs of the people of this State. Once elected, you'll be able to reach my cabinet and speak with them and hear from them directly as well. We have needed to hold our officiants responsible for some time now and have not been able to. I promise that once elected, they will answer to *you* so a tragesty like this will never, *ever,* happen again."

"You heard it here first folks, Leonard Steel will be making decisions based on *your* recommendations, not career scientists, or career politicians, people with agendas of their own," Tanner said with a flourish.

Guru Geena hit pause on the recording.

Johanna propped her elbow on the conference room table, pinching her forehead with her fingertips, turning to Rashmi to say, "This can't be happening, all the free advertising, people will be talking about him nonstop from now until Election Day."

"Governor Fanning can't compete with that," Rashmi agreed.

# Chapter Fifteen

It had been Neil. Dinner was canceled. The leeches all took off moments after she had answered up the phone. He had told them first. While she was on the phone Gayatri had peeked through the vertical blinds and watched her father's friends gather their belongings, leaving their trash behind on the wooden tables and benches before heading to their vehicles. She bit her nails nervously after Kavita hung up the phone and stood there silently with her lips pressed tight. Gayatri had been watching her Aunt Kavita all afternoon and didn't want to be another person who disappointed her.

Kavita thought she could hear the blood pounding in her ears. She had wanted one custom for their family to keep in tradition and Neil thought nothing of it. Kavita felt the veins in her own neck as she thought about how Neil thought nothing of her. She drew the cord on the vertical blinds so she could look for herself and saw what she had expected. Empty piles of trash. Neil had put Alfie and the leeches before Gayatri and before her. Now they were long gone and all that was left was a mess.

Kavita wanted to rip the blinds off the wall. To destroy the kitchen. She hadn't even gotten to ask him what his plan was for Gayatri's birthday party. He had hung up on her. It wasn't even on his mind.

"Nick needs me to do something, we won't be needing dinner tonight, and heads up, we're gonna need you and the girls at the march, Nick said Steel wants women showing their support," was what he did have the time to say.

All Kavita did was cook and clean for her brother, all day every day. Take care of his daughters. His friends. And she meant nothing to him no matter what she did. She was just his servant.

Kavita did not want Gayatri to see her so upset like this. She would pretend everything was ok, because when she didn't, she started to fall apart. She couldn't fall apart. Not yet.

"Are you hungry beti? Shall we eat? Just the two of us tonight, that will be nice, won't it?" As she acted for Gayatri, Kavita realized this was what she actually preferred. She was always forcing the dinner table to be special for Gayatri but tonight it would be. She wouldn't have to entertain Neil. Or brag about Gayatri to her own father.

"I have a story for you now," Gayatri said as they sat across from one another.

"Oh?" Kavita was pleased.

"Yeah, I know about Abhaya Mudra," Gayatri began, "It is my favorite one. It means we can be free from fear and that we come in peace."

"That's right!" Kavita agreed proudly.

"That was my only story," Gayatri admitted and Kavita laughed and clapped for her niece. She was honored that Gayatri had wanted to share what she knew with her.

"Well, your story reminds me of a good one. Would you listen to it for me? It's about having no fear, even if we love to be scared," Kavita looked to Gayatri and saw her continued eating as wanting to be entertained, so she began, "One day, Durga's tiger friend and lion friend were playing in Saaya's forest. They kept ending in a tie. They'd tell one another 'best two out of three matches', but then the other would win and they would change it to whoever won three out of five would be given the title of *Best Cat*. On and on until Durga told them they had had enough play arguments for the day and that they had to get on their way. The silly billies would keep saying, 'just one more match!' until Durga had had enough. She canceled their plans and changed all three of their appearances, so they would no longer be seen as Durga, her tiger, and her lion but simply three friends, traveling through town.

"'Chalo,' Durga commanded, and her friends followed her, walking slightly behind her as they felt ashamed knowing Durga had grown impatient with them.

"Durga took her friends out of Saaya's lush green forest and traveled down the dusty road with them. They made their way to the town's market where they walked through rows of stalls selling produce, jams, jellies, breads, chutneys, and even a vendor selling jars of Queen Shahad's honeys. The three friends stopped to watch some jugglers entertain shoppers and passed a group of musicians packing up their instruments on stage. Durga continued on in her disguise and the two feline friends lost her for a bit when they got distracted by a dog begging for treats where shoppers gathered to take rest, sipping their chai and devouring their purchased snacks.

"The three friends traveled through the market this way. The two felines kept stopping to take in all of the scents of the market, there were so many people and so many goods with fragrances to inventory. Once they realized Durga was farther ahead of them, they would rush to continue on their journey, running to be the first one to catch up to her. They called no attention to themselves as they traveled through the market this way. It was a chaotic place with many people making their way hurriedly, children calling for their parents if lost or to buy them things, and shopkeepers yelling above the crowds, instructing them to stop shopping where there were to check out the *best* prices in the market. But eventually, they made their way through the busy market with Durga indicating they had finally arrived as she stood holding the flap of a canvas tent open. She greeted her companions as they caught up with sheepish looks in their eyes. Durga smiled gently as them before saying, 'You want to know who is the best? Who is number one? Step inside and we can settle this with one last fight.'

"The two felines looked at one another, gently accepted the other's paw and stepped inside. Durga had led them to the artist's gallery, where patrons stood silently admiring all of the creativity on display. Durga traversed the people gazing with wonder at sculptures, illustrations, pottery, and more as her friends continued to follow behind, eventually making their way to a merchant whose art held the gaze of none. The merchant welcomed the three friends loudly, waving his arms, beckoning them to take a closer look at his goods.

"Durga and her felines, hidden by their disguises, stood admiring his stall, which was covered entirely with the most beautiful paintings. All of cats.

"Durga pointed to the first painting she saw, it was of Saaya. Saaya was hidden behind tall blades of amber feathergrass, his black fur poked through, and his green eyes shone, brightly. All of the colors of the landscape contrasting with the bright blue sky that held a sun shining its rays down onto Saaya, creating a royal crown for the feline.

"'How much for that one?' Durga asked the merchant.

"'Oh, this tiny panther is a beloved resident. This painting is so valuable, I'm not sure I can even part with it.'

"Durga looked around to point out to the merchant that he had no other buyers interested in the art he was trying to sell. The merchant squinted his eyes at Durga and then his shoulders slumped as he told her, 'Ok, for a quality customer like you I will sell it for 28 gold pieces. Or I would trade you the painting for your beautiful cloak,' the merchant said as he attempted to examine the cloak's embroidery from his side of the stall.

"Durga gave a nod that was neither a yes or a no and then pointed to the two paintings surrounding the one of Saaya. One was Durga's lion, standing tall and proud. His mane blowing in the wind, as he stood upon a mountaintop. The lion was painted in such a way that when you looked at it, Durga's lion friend looked back at you sharing a look with smile that made you think the two of you held a secret bond.

"The second painting was of Durga's tiger, her stripes beautifully represented as she hid in camouflage, her paws extended in front of her as she posed relaxed, in front of a large blue lake. There were dozens of birds in the painting. Some drank directly from the lake while others hovered above the surface as the tiger reclined in her jungle home. As the three friends examined the painting they saw other birds hiding in the branches of the tree, studying the powerful cat. The birds working together as they kept watch and hydrated, keeping one another safe from the huntress.

"'And how much for each of those two paintings? The lion or the tiger?' Durga asked the merchant.

"'Those two paintings?' the merchant asked back as he scratched out his ear, assuming he had to have misheard his potential customer.

"Durga looked at the merchant expectantly and when he saw that her inquiry was genuine, he responded, 'If you purchase the painting of the black panther, you'll have such good luck I will just throw the other two in for free.'

"Durga agreed immediately to the merchant's offer and with gratitude gave him the cloak he so admired. Her companions helped the merchant pack up the paintings and under their breath kept muttering things to one another such as 'How could that tiny panther be worth 28 gold pieces and we are worth nothing?' and 'He must've just been so desperate to get rid of his inventory that he was ready to give his paintings away!', careful to hush if they saw Durga was nearby.

"'We aren't on the path to the mountains or to the jungles,' she commented as together they shed their disguises. As they walked along the dirt path, the two felines forgot they had gotten in trouble and began to wrestle with one another. The two friends had fun as they took turns running ahead to hide in the grasses and then pouncing, surprising Durga so much she jumped, or chasing one another's tails until they ended up in summersaults and she bubbled with delight and how they played. Durga scritched her friends' scruff and told them how much they meant to her.

"'If you stand with the knowledge of your own worth, you'll never have to prove yourself to another. Be fearless and know that you are enough. Release you desire to be the best. Your radiance will shine when you know there is no competition. The lion learns from the tiger and the tiger learns from the lion. We can learn from Saaya, and we can teach Saaya. If we come in peace,' Durga told her friends as they traveled along the road with their paintings."

Kavita looked to Gayatri, and then up to Durga. She felt as though she could finally breathe. Kavita accepted that this was the first time in quite a long time, that she felt unrestrained and unafraid.

# Chapter Sixteen

Anand saw the earth beginning to shift and bulge. His rhythms had merged with the earth's and synchronized with the heavens. His water bottle had slowly begun to fill with rainwater and the men had come to march.

Anand tipped his head back to listen as he played his song with the elements. He kept his eyes shut as he heard Neil's voice, leading the call. Anand began to feel weightless as the song played on. A hawk cried and he snapped to attention, realizing he was no longer percussive. He stood with his feet wide and was holding his arms out to the sky; swaying to the music in the shape of an X. Anand felt the magic pulling at him, taking advantage of his distraction.

The magic wasn't his. Anand was sure of that now. It would take advantage of him to in order to take advantage of this situation. Anand would float away if he didn't focus. He had to get to the compound. But song of the militia calling to him and the elements were telling him to join back in. Over the past few years his brother had tried to persuade him to join, told him to join, and each time Anand had refused. Anand would refuse once more. After this last song.

And so, Anand used his talent, his tempo leading Neil's call.

*I said one day I wanna be*
*One of Lenny's deputies*
*I showed up, I feel no pain*
*I march on in cold and rain*

Anand felt the wind stir and listened as a few dead branches pattered to the forest carpet from the gust. Their fall propelling him.

*I said one day I wanna be | One of Lenny's deputies*
*I showed up, I feel no pain | I march on in cold and rain*

The men practicing their formation for the Salute to Straights Parade began to quicken their pace. Anand's arms moved faster, the beat moved on, and the men marching called back to Neil:

*I said one day I wanna be| One of Lenny's deputies | I showed up, I feel no pain| I march on in cold and rain*

Anand heard the squall of a random bird as some of the younger trees of the forest joined the song, adding their groans and moans as the wind picked up, pushing them to move faster too. On and on this went. Back and forth between Anand and the men in the militia. To and fro between the humans and nature. Anand's arms kept up, but they were beginning to tire from pumping the rhythm. The men were enjoying the song and dance, their voices full of pleasure of pride as they sang their call to one another. As they spun on each side of the bridge to start again each pushed the other to quicken the song's tempo.

*I said one day I wanna be | One of Lenny's deputies | I showed up, I feel no pain | I march on in cold and rain | I said one day I wanna be | One of Lenny's deputies | I showed up, I feel no pain | I march on in cold and rain | I said one day I wanna be | One of Lenny's deputies | I showed up, I feel no pain |I march on in cold and rain | I said one day I wanna be | One of Lenny's deputies | I showed up, I feel no pain | I march on in cold and rain | I said one day I wanna be | One of Lenny's deputies | I showed up, I feel no pain | I march on in cold and rain | I said one day I wanna be | One of Lenny's deputies | I showed up, I feel no pain |I march on in cold and rain*

Anand was certain he was not seeing anything. He blinked open his eyes wide over and over. He did not want to stop his contribution to the song, worried it would allow the magic to take over, so he began to strike a log with his wizard's staff, and wiped his eyes clear with the other. He could see the bridge wobbling once again. The trailing movements were visible to Anand's eyes, how was it possible that Neil and the men could not see the bridge's movement?

*Isaidonedaylwannabe|OneofLenny'sdeputies|Ishowedup,Ifeelnopain|Imarchonincoldandrain|I saidonedaylwannabe|OneofLenny'sdeputies|Ishowedup,Ifeelnopain|Imarchonincoldandrain|Is*

Tears spilled down Anand's face as a wail escaped. He had no control of this or any magic. It was the men causing the oscillation of the bridge. It was the bridge causing the men to march faster. Anand knew it wasn't his magic because when he moved to wipe his eyes, he had slowed his own song. He willed the men to go slower as he struck the log, but he could not slow them down. They would not slow down. The men fell in step with the bridge's vibration. The vibration called on the men to march faster and faster, daring them to keep up.

Anand had stopped drumming entirely, his heart in his stomach, he felt like nothing was real, but that nothing could be more real than this. He crumpled down to the earth, he had lost all strength in his legs and felt himself curl into a fern once more. Anand told himself that if his magic was real that he would sacrifice himself to the earth to make it all stop. He squeezed himself tight, expecting the earth to allow him to shrink into her. Anand laid there curled up, waiting to be cradled by the earth long after he heard the thunder crack. The earth rejected him and so he embraced himself. Just as he knew there was no magic, he knew there had been no thunderbolt of lightning. The piercing boom Anand had heard was that of the Canary Canyon bridge collapse.

# Chapter Seventeen

Rashmi sat with the other women, lost in her own thoughts. Tanner's interview with Steel had made her feel worse the longer it went on. Guru Geena had to pause the recording multiple times as the other women lost their patience, booing at the screen. It made the whole viewing take up more time than it had to, however they felt about it, Guru Geena was sure that the women would not miss the next horrible thing he went on to say. After the announcement of his pro-Steel propaganda station, he lectured the viewers on the dangers of listening to news and editorials from people you didn't know and couldn't verify hadn't put a spin on their reporting.

"The great people who live here deserve to hear directly from me, just like we're doing right now," Steel told Tanner, "Now, no offense to you Tanner, but you didn't grow up here. So, who are you to really ask *me* about what it's like to have grown up here, go to school here, become the businessman that I am today, and to *return* here to help the great people of this state that I love. That have been taken advantage of for too long. Other people, *outsiders,* coming in, trying to tell us what's best and we just don't need that. Hear it straight from me, there's no need for anyone to interpret anything."

"Yeah, he'll lie straight to your face," Johanna muttered, prompting Guru Geena to ask if she was hearing a request for another pause. The recording played on as Rashmi agreed with Johanna. Steel was a great liar and a great denier. Rashmi hated how he walked this earth with nothing to fear.

Rashmi expected another pause seeing the women look at one another in horror as Steel announced his next pledge. "28% of the men in this great State filed for unemployment. These are great men who want to work. They have something to offer, and I genuinely believe that. That's why I'm proud to announce that *Strong as Steel TV* is for the people. I am offering these men opportunities to work directly for me, Leonard Steel."

Tanner was grinning, and began to gesture wildly with excitement, "Tell us more about these jobs you are creating."

The footage changed back to Nick, on scene at the supermarket where the attack had taken place. Nick was standing with his legs slightly apart, holding his hands behind his back, chest puffed out to look important, making up for the fact that he had nothing left to do now that all the water had been handed out. The recording returned to a split screen of the two men and Steel went on, "Men can apply to work on infrastructure projects the way Huber Consultants did with the men right here. Nick, who we just saw, is a businessman just like me. A man who cares about his neighbors, his town, his state. One of us. He saw there was a need in his town, a pedestrian bridge to build connection to some of the most scenic views in Shepherd County. On his own Nick found men who also wanted to make this place better. We all got together and got it done for a fraction of the price the State would have charged. We hope to work with business owners like Nick, all across the State to improve our own lives. No one else can help us. But for us to get this done, before time runs out, I do need to your vote," Steel pointed at the camera, directly at The Ladoo Crew watching the recording.

To Rashmi, Tanner's eyes and smile all worked together to create the face of a fanatic. Rashmi figured Tanner must be obsessed with Steel as she watched him spurting worship, dropping the façade of the interview and directly prompting his guest, "So there's been rumors here that you will be personally paying out of pocket for *multiple* opportunities for the unemployed, not just infrastructure in their own communities. Is the rumor true? Will you be hiring Steel Campaign Content Creators?"

"The rumors are true Tanner," Steel said, as though Tanner had just paid him a compliment, "I will be paying residents $600 per month to help us get those votes, creating additional jobs, which you can do right in your own home."

"What would these 'work from home' jobs be exactly?" Tanner asked.

"We need help managing our content, our communities, you would be getting paid to post on social media several times a day about your support for our campaign, things you are doing already," Steel smiled at Tanner and the viewers watching, "Best of all you'll get a social media badge verifying you as *Strong as Steel* and will get a discount on all Slater Corporation entertainment services."

"And I hate to ask, but my producer, she's a woman and she told me I had to ask," Tanner waggled his finger at the camera so everyone would know what a nag his producer was, asking Steel, "Would any of these positions be available to women?"

"Of course!" Steel laughed, "We encourage anyone who can *legally* work to apply. The hiring for infrastructure jobs would be left to the local business owners, like Nick over there, so anyone who can prove they can do the work could get to work as soon as those contracts are awarded.

"We particularly encourage women to apply to work in our content creation department. I've spoken with many mothers throughout my campaign, many who are really struggling to get food on the table, or need help getting child support from the fathers of their children. With such a high unemployment rate, how could these men possibly pay? I'm running for governor to help all the people in this great State. Especially the children, we must look out for them."

"I was just about to ask you about that, CEO Steel," Tanner was back to full screen.

"Tanner's bitch of a producer must have nagged him to continue his hosting duties," Rashmi joked quietly enough that Guru Geena didn't hear but she got a couple of snorts from Norah.

"Meeting with families across this state I couldn't believe how many lived such hectic lives. So far apart. Multiple jobs, splitting kids between homes and their own relatives. I spoke with many fathers who barely saw their children. I couldn't believe it and reached out to my team to find out why. What I learned stunned me Tanner. There is so much owed child support. And how couldn't there be? Mothers need help raising their children and fathers need to pay for their own homes once their family has been taken from them. Who can afford to live that way? And why isn't anything being done about it? There is a way to prioritize helping these families out!

"You know Tanner, right there in Shepherd County I spoke to a man whose ex is withholding visitation from his two daughters because he owes her too much money. His ex is saying that his daughters are worth a certain amount of money, and until she has that money, he can't see them. I thought that was absolutely horrible, the thought of not being able to see my own children. Every day I thank the good lord that I married a decent wife. He fit me with a good woman." Steel took a short pause and then continued after a few moments of faking the appropriate emotional response, "This man is a good man, who worked hard constructing the new bridge in Shepherd County and just wanted his daughters to be able to see one another. I paid his child support off myself and spoke with his ex, who promised me she will allow him to be with his daughters together this weekend, at a family birthday party. The first they've all been at together since his oldest was born, this good man told me.

"If there are other women who are withholding their children from their fathers, for just a few bucks, these jobs will help these men out. Whether they encourage their exes to apply for them or whether they apply for themselves. We at Slater Corporation have a saying, *we help those who help themselves*. If these mothers are so upset at not getting paid enough to raise their children, they can look to see if they are taking every opportunity afforded to them. Heck, for a two-parent household, with my proposed eight pm curfew, a family could make an extra $1200 a month once the kids were asleep. If they have children over 14 who want to work, that income increases even more. Is Governess Fanning able to propose that?"

"Well, it sounds like you have a plan to really improve these citizens' lives CEO Steel," Tanner began to wrap the interview up, "Thank you for joining us tonight."

"Thank you for having me, and thank *you*," Steel spoke directly to the viewers once again, "for all you do to make this State and our country great. There's no better place to live, because of you. Let's continue to improve our lives and if anyone doesn't like it, they can leave!"

At that Guru Geena paused the recording and the room buzzed with the announcement of Steel's propaganda machine. So much speculation and so much emotion, many women were scared about what this meant for their futures.

Rashmi thought about her past. All her mother had been through and fought for, and how one man could wipe it all away. Rashmi chuckled to herself, with spite. If one man could wipe it all away, Rashmi would still do what she could about it.

"Men are snowflakes that can easily ride the wind and travel far from their responsibilities; you can try to catch them, but they hide in ice or will melt and disappear. If men wanted children of their own, they'd have them; hire childcare, chefs, pay laboratory fees to have a child on their own. Raise them. I have never seen a man pay for that when they can get the dudh for free. We women, we are snowflakes, but from ice we become water, then vapor, we fall from the clouds, again and again, on and on," Anjali had told Rashmi, that summer after her own father's death, when she had been complaining as she was being forced to take IILS.

Rashmi knew her mother had been grateful to her own parents for encouraging her own studies to the degree that they had, Anjali had to help her own mother raise her younger brothers so they got good grades and stayed out of trouble. *Boys will be boys.* If they got good grades, then Rashmi's grandparents would be taken care of in their old age. Unfortunately, Anjali had never realized that her sacrifice meant nothing to her own mother and father. It was expected of her so there was not much gratitude there. If Anjali complained, Nani told her that it was her obligation for being born. Nana and Nani had gambled and invested all their money and parenting towards their sons. A gamble they lost in Rashmi's opinion, because their brightest child, Anjali, moved to the States as soon as she could. Maybe things would have been different for Anjali if she had grown up hearing her parents tell her younger brothers, 'Quit playing! Be more responsible like your sister.' But Anjali had only ever heard, 'Anjali, no time for play! Be more responsible and help out.' Anjali's duty was to do it all. Take care of everyone. To anticipate what others needed. And she had been replaced by another so easily once her little brother got married. There was novelty for her parents, they could make someone new work even harder for their respect and love.

Anjali had never once opined negatively about Rashmi's Nana and Nani to her daughter. Anjali had raised Rashmi to think a similar way, duty first. Yet Rashmi saw her mother's strength, how she did so much with so little. It was hard for Rashmi to begin to comprehend how her mother was so accepting of the conditions she had been raised in. *That's just how the world works. It is what it is, beti.*

Rashmi did not know her grandparents, so it came easy to her to dislike them. Resent them for making Anjali hard on Rashmi. Knowing that her own mother could be casually replaced by someone else's daughter made her glad to have never met them. And then to watch their daughter travel halfway across the globe with a man they barely knew. Rashmi often thought about how lonely her mother must have been but didn't dwell on the topic; she knew much more about how thrilled her mother had been as well.

Anjali had grown up in such a different culture from Rashmi. She harbored no ill will towards her own parents although she was aware of the disdain her daughter had for them. That hadn't been Anjali's intention. She had simply wanted Rashmi to know how good she had it when she made major decisions about her life. *It could be worse, beti.* Her hope was that Rashmi could imagine Anjali at age 14 and how she would have never believed the freedom she would one day have. Anjali's opinion was that her parents did their best. *It could be worse, beti.* Sons were always more important in their culture, it is how they had grown up and so, that was how Anjali had. *It is what it is, beti.* Anjali could not fault her parents; they believed that Bhagwan would provide for them if they followed the rules, and they were right. Anjali was the eldest sister to three smart, little brothers. Anjali had been smarter than any of her brothers but that had never mattered. *That's just how the world works. It is what it is, beti.* It was expected of her to be better than them, and at the same time, to be rarely acknowledged and often dismissed. *Wait for your turn beti, let your brothers go first, you'll see its better this way.*

Anjali had to be smart enough to take care of her brothers. And her elders. But it was never expected that she would take care of herself. Anjali's brothers would get good marks, get good careers, and their family's investment would pay off as they got older, while their wives and daughters took excellent care of Nana and Nani. Anjali would get good marks, make good rotis, help her mother keep a clean house, make sure her brothers got good grades, and then get married and help take care of her husband's family. *That's just how the world works, wait your turn, it is what it is, beti.*

By chance, Anjali somehow managed to break tradition, liberated from the duty that had been assigned to her by her own mother when she was born once her husband had passed. That led to Rashmi's freedom in adulthood. *Don't worry about your turn beti, wait, let your brothers go first, that's just how the world works, you'll see its better this way.* When Anjali had been a young girl, she resolved to destroy their family's ancient custom if given the chance. With no declaration Anjali simply released an arrow into motion, knowing its trajectory could never be preset.

Rashmi thought of 14-year-old Anjali, so reliable as the eldest daughter in her family. Young Anjali never being able to offer an excuse if she overlooked one of her responsibilities. Anjali who had always picked up the slack when others didn't follow through. Rashmi held back tears as she imagined her mother being told to make 'Steel for Governor' memes for $600 a month, so that her brothers could have

114

more than she could ever see herself having. To make their Steel Campaign posts for them because her younger brothers needed more time to rest and study.

Rashmi had always had a hard time accepting *it is what it is.*

# Chapter Eighteen

Kavita and Gayatri had packed up all the leftovers and thoroughly cleaned the kitchen. Kavita had wanted to toss it all in the trash. She had spent all day cooking, there was a birthday party she wasn't invited to tomorrow where the leeches would all feast, and there was the Salute to Straights Parade the day after that. She'd be eating this tomato curry for the next week, she had made so much.

She was done with this day. As soon as she put Gayatri to bed she would tuck herself in. Sleep was the only thing she craved. No more chores. She had thought about waiting up to confront Neil about the birthday party but decided it wasn't worth it. If he didn't want her there, what was the point? She didn't want to be there either.

Gayatri had completed her bedtime routine and approached Kavita to get tucked in. Kavita obliged and scooted in beside her. As she laid on her side, she began Gayatri's bedtime story, "Durga spins the Sudarshan Chakra on her finger, it never touches her, it spins perfectly without touching any part of her hand, for her essence is that where creation is balanced with righteousness so all may be free from oppression. The disc will spin forever, on and on time goes, just as our quest for balance will go on forever.

"Back in Saaya's forest, a young mouse named Mathieu ran through the grasses as a red-tailed hawk named Harvey chased him. Mathieu found a rabbit's burrow and asked if he could hide there, to escape Harvey's pursuit. The rabbits living there agreed and when Harvey came pecking at their entrance, they shouted at the hawk to go away and respect their guest, Mathieu. But Harvey refused, causing an uproar after being told he was not welcome. Harvey clawed and flapped his feathers, making himself madder and madder as he realized causing such a disturbance had made all the prey he would normally hunt run away. This made Harvey even more angry, and in a rage, he destroyed the rabbits' den. Some of the rabbits in the family were able to run away, managing to survive but the hawk killed many, along with their guest, the small mouse named Mathieu.

"A 13-lined ground squirrel, her name was Scarlett, had been awaiting her friend Mathieu's arrival that afternoon. She went looking for him and saw the ruckus Harvey brought to the plains where the rabbits lived. She stood watching this commotion all afternoon and could not believe this one hawk had ruined so many lives, spilling the blood of Mathieu and the rabbits in such a gruesome process. So much needless violence because Harvey felt he had been humiliated. Scarlett feared the hawk would continue this behavior amongst the animals of the forest so watched the hawk, following him all the way home to his nest. When Harvey and his wife left their nest unattended Scarlett climbed up and rolled every single one of the hawks' eggs out, and then ran away, as fast as possible.

"The hawks were devastated but were used to this retaliation so moved their nest a few branches up. They knew that mice and smaller rodents that would be friends of Mathieu, such as Scarlett the 13-lined ground squirrel, could not climb so high. But they did not know that the rodents did not just keep to themselves, they could never survive if they did that. To protect one another, they had for a long time worked together with many animals in Saaya's forest, and the story of Harvey's attack made it to the raccoons, who were able to climb high.

"The raccoons worried that their homes could be easily destroyed by the hawks, but they knew if they did nothing, they would be destroyed so they followed Scarlett's lead. They took a vote and decided that when the hawks next left their nest, the raccoons would send their bravest climber, Rafael, up the tree to roll the hawk eggs out, one by one.

"The hawks were devastated once again, this time by Rafael and the others who stood watch so that he could safely get to the hawk's nest and back, reporting that he had completed his mission. Harvey and his wife could not place their nest any higher in a tree because the raccoons were such expert climbers and now had the aid of many of the creatures of the forest keeping watch on the hawks. Harvey, along with his wife went to Durga, telling her that they were being bullied out of the forest. The hawks asked Durga if she would keep their nest safe in the pack of one of her feline companions. Durga agreed, sad that there was this imbalance in the forest. She offered the tiger's pack to protect the hawk's nest.

"However, a sparrow named Saffa had spied this interaction and reported back to the rest of the creatures of the forest. Saffa was furious at how Harvey had lied to Durga, omitting the fact that it was the hawk himself who had caused the initial upset in the forest. All the animals were confused as to what to do. Saffa's voice trembled as she was petrified to speak about the horrors Harvey and his wife had committed against her family and friends, sabotaging them each spring as they tried to care for their young, and though they hadn't done anything right then, and though she was afraid now, Saffa vowed to challenge Durga's tiger friend to destroy the hawks' nest.

"With great determination and clutching the teeniest of branches in her claws, Saffa flew to Durga and her companions. She landed on the tiger's scruff and slid the branch underneath the tiger's pack. The tiger felt the tickle, that tickle turning into a scratch. When the tiger could not stand the scratch any longer, the tiger shifted all of her weight, shaking and flapping the pack off her body, destroying the eggs in the hawks' nest at once.

"Durga had to console the hawks' and apologize on behalf of the tiger, who should have asked for help or to be scratched rather than react by throwing the pack off her back. The hawks were wailing, asking Durga how she could have done this to them, pleading with her to make the creatures of the forest stop their mistreatment of them.

"At this Saaya hopped down from the tree where they had been eavesdropping and told Durga and her feline companions everything, knowing they would protect Saaya from the same hawks who had chased him through the forest at many different times of day, on many different occasions. Saaya told Durga that the rabbits had offered protection to Mathieu and rather than leaving, Harvey destroyed everything, even after murdering poor Mathieu, who had only been trying to meet his friend.

"At this Durga felt her heart hurt, she had protected the hawks knowing there was an imbalance and blood being shed. Durga had just scolded her tiger friend for not asking for help, but she had not been paying attention to who really needed help herself. She promised all of the creatures she would not allow this to happen ever again. And so, she punished the red-tailed hawks, scolding them for disrespecting the rabbits' request of peace for their guest. Durga warned the hawks that from now on, whenever they went hunting, they would be chased out by mobs of other animals. The hawks had had it easy for so long and even that had not been enough for them; the hawks had wanted more; taking that which had not belonged to them had caused an imbalance in the forest."

Kavita looked over at Gayatri, seeing her eyes open and shut as she fought off sleep. Kavita kissed her niece on the forehead and then left her bedroom once she had fully fallen asleep. She would teach her about Durga's sword of wisdom and tell her The Tale of Saaya's curse as she cooked Gayatri her birthday breakfast. She would show her beloved how unique fights require unique weapons.

# Epilogue

It hadn't taken a torrential rain to erode parts of the earth. Just some rain falling where the soil was thin. Neil was watching it all around him as he laid at the bottom of Canary Canyon. The pain was unlike anything he had ever felt in his life. Just a few hours ago Nick had promised him it had been safe, to stop worrying after Neil had reported that the bridge had felt unsteady during practice. And then tonight when it had begun again, Neil's friends in the militia had leaned into it, laughing and trying to get the bridge to vibrate even more. Nick tried to command them to stop, yelling at them to stop fucking around, to take AmBackPats seriously. They yelled back, telling him to stop being such a pussy. To lighten up. Neil had wanted them to listen to him and for them to accept him and his rank. They'd be forced to accept him when Nick appointed him General of Shepherd County AmBackPats. He was watching Nick rise in Steel's ranks, meaning he had to be the one Nick depended on so that he rose with him. But Nick was never there doing the hard work Neil did, he just got all the glory. Neil was sick of doing all Nick's hard work, so he joined the other men, shouting, "Let's bring the ruckus boys!"

Which they did, causing the bridge to rock and sway. Marching, calling, whistling, laughing, composing music until they fell to meet the rocks waiting for them in the small stream at the bottom of the ravine. *I showed up, I feel no pain.*

There should have been 30 of them. Marching in rows of four, Neil in the back. Nick, self-appointed Chief of AmBackPats, was supposed to be leading in front, but he'd only shown up to practice a handful of times. Steel had told Nick that Slater TV would be streaming the march on multiple stations and Nick wanted to be sure he'd be seen as the leader with this formation when Steel spoke. But right now Nick wasn't there, he had been called to do something more important and told Neil to lead one final practice march. Neil was eager to please, each time Nick was absent, Neil looked like a leader to the other men. It would make it easier for them to accept his appointment as General. Besides, sacrifices had to be made for Steel to win. Missing one dinner with his daughter wasn't that big of a deal. Nick had promised him a big party at his club tomorrow, he would probably announce Neil's appointment as General then. It also doubled as a convenient spot for Gaya's birthday party, a good way for Nick to drum up business - having the men pitch in for drinks when the tab came; Kavita could organize the potluck how she always did, she loved cooking at home. And there'd be even more patrons at Nick's Club with the expected Salute to Straights turnout the day after. That's why Nick was in charge, he had the ideas and Neil was learning a lot from the Chief.

Neil looked around him, the men all writhing in pain, laying as the water rushed around them. He had felt the wind gusting when they marched above and somehow, laying deep below the bridge he still felt it all around him, the chill causing his teeth to chatter. Canary Creek was still low, only a foot or two deep but the water was moving fast as the storm continued to grow stronger. They had to get out of there as quickly as they could. Neil was lucky Nick had planned this at the beginning of the season as opposed to leaving it until a few weeks later. Breaking bones crashing into rocks was better than being swept away, right?

Neil dragged himself onto his side and reached into his pocket to grab his mobile. He looked and saw no bars. He tried to get on all fours to crawl and was barely able to. That had taken all of his strength. He would never be able to make his way up the slick, rocky ledges of the bank without help. And who knows how long it would be before help arrived. He laid there panting as he looked around and saw his men were all in the same shape, some in pain, many in agony, barely able to drag themselves on their bellies against the rocks and deadfall as the frigid water flowed past.

Neil realized help may be on the way. The women living on this land had security cameras, Nick had pointed them out to him when they first surveyed the land to build the bridge. They called themselves The Ladoo Crew and hid behind security fencing. What a fucking joke.

Neil laid there, holding back his emotions, he was still in front of the other men, no matter how much he wanted to wail in pain. Drops of rain plunked from the sky, joining the tears silently streaming down his face. Neil closed his eyes and felt his breath through his bruised and broken ribs. While Neil laid at the bottom of Canary Canyon, he felt the air pressure drop and watched the sky turn into deeper and darker shadows.

As Neil felt the storm surging, the rage that had been in his belly for ages began to seethe, and then leaked out, surrounding him. "Those Ladoo Crew bitches better rescue us soon!" he demanded, howling to the men he had been waiting to lead.

# Acknowledgements

'Azaadi' has been used as a call and response chant by South Asian feminists for decades, first by Pakistani feminists who were not allowed to meet and organize, but did so however they could, with chants such as:

Aurat ka naara
[azaadi]
Bachchan ka naara
[azaadi]
Hum leke rahenge
[azaadi]
Hai pyaara naara
[azaadi]


Women want freedom
Children want freedom
We will take our freedom
We will love our freedom

The call and response grew after Kamla Bhasin recited it at a Women's Studies Conference in the early '90s. Poetry such as:

From patriarchy
[azaadi]
From all hierarchy
[azaadi]
From endless violence
[azaadi]
From helpless silence
[azaadi]
For walking freely

[azaadi]
For talking freely
[azaadi]
For dancing madly
[azaadi]
For singing loudly
[azaadi]
For self-expression
[azaadi]
For celebration
[azaadi]
We love it madly
[azaadi]
Come say it loudly!
[AZAADI!]

I am including a link to an interview by TheQuint.com with Kamla Bhasin if you are interested in learning more about this history and how this chant is one that is alive and evolving in order to include the struggles of so many, so all can be free: https://youtu.be/Ez7pFJqoSP8

When I was a young girl, I fell in love with cats. I would go to the library every Saturday with my mom and sit in the reference section, reading everything that I could about them. I remember being very young and my dad was getting ready for a trip to India. He asked me what I wanted him to bring back as a gift and everyone laughed at me when I told him I wanted a cat. I didn't get one, but I did get a Garfield stuffed animal, which I loved, that Christmas.

When I was living on my own, I was finally able to adopt cats and we had years of friendship together. Mittens and Marvel lived with me until they were seniors, and I was so grateful to have experienced life with them. The three of us kind of grew together and over time I realized how much cats were disliked as they were viewed with some sort of feminine association. Cat fights, catcalls, cats are sensitive and easily scared, cats are so proper, always cleaning themselves, a cat does not like being put on a leash, and most aren't fond of wearing those little collars with bells. Cats don't assume that you deserve their attention and exactly what kind of person would want to live with all that?

I'd like to thank my friend EM for telling me she thought I was ready to adopt new friends, encouraging me as she reminded me how much love I have in my heart. I need to thank my friend AJ for sending me photos of kitties, and of course, BG for allowing two new roomies to move into our home. I have so much gratitude to MH for teaching me about lifelines. AM thank you for editing this book and telling me that I didn't need to try because I'm doing. I love you JS for writing with me and encouraging me to keep going. Thank you, SZ & MM, for letting me talk about this book all day.

I have no thank you big enough for the Tejal Yoga Community for inviting me to speak on Sci-fi, Yoga, & Liberation while I was writing this book. Thank you for amplifying South Asian voices, creating community, and modeling inclusivity.

And finally, thank you Marceline & Elroy for being great cats, telling me what words to put down where, which windows to open, where I should sit, and most importantly, when to take rest.

Made in the USA
Monee, IL
19 November 2024

70589870R00075